The Golden Quest

THE FOUR VOYAGES OF
CHRISTOPHER COLUMBUS

Michael Anthony

CARIBBEAN

First published 1992

Published by THE MACMILLAN PRESS LTD
London and Basingstoke
*Associated companies and representatives in Accra,
Auckland, Delhi, Dublin, Gaborone, Hamburg, Harare,
Hong Kong, Kuala Lumpur, Lagos, Manzini, Melbourne,
Mexico City, Nairobi, New York, Singapore, Tokyo*

ISBN 0-333-56868-0

Printed in Hong Kong

A catalogue record for this book is available from
the British Library.

Acknowledgements
The authors and publishers wish to acknowledge, with thanks, the following
photographic sources.
Mary Evans Picture Library pp30; 55; 57; 106; 198   Hulton-Deutsch
Collection pp3; 24; 49; 93; 111; 140   Peter Newark's Historical Pictures pp64;
196   Peter Newark's Western Americana Pictures pp38; 47
The cover picture is courtesy of Peter Newark's Western Americana Pictures.
The publishers have made every effort to trace the copyright holders, but if they
have inadvertently overlooked any, they will be pleased to make the necessary
arrangements at the first opportunity.

Contents

To Jennifer, Keith, Carlos and Sandra

Other books by Michael Anthony

Fiction

The Games Were Coming
The Year in San Fernando
Green Days by the River
Cricket in the Road
Streets of Conflict
Folktales and Fantasies
King of the Masquerade
Bright Road to El Dorado
All That Glitters

Non-fiction

Profile Trinidad
Glimpses of Trinidad and Tobago
The Making of Port-of-Spain
Port-of-Spain in a World at War
First in Trinidad
Heroes of the People of Trinidad and Tobago
A Better and a Brighter Day
Towns and Villages of Trinidad and Tobago
Parade of the Carnivals

Author's Note

In looking into the four voyages of Christopher Columbus one has to be as objective as possible if one is born in the Americas, and especially so in the West Indies. All West Indian school-children have grown up regarding Christopher Columbus as a towering figure of history. And yet, ironically, they know so little about this Genoese. How many Jamaican children know, for instance, of the interesting and colourful part Jamaica played in the exploration by Columbus on the fourth voyage? How many school-children from Guadeloupe know of the bizarre days Columbus and his men spent on their island? And to look at the case of Trinidad – much of what school-children know of the Columbus connection is false. Indeed, we can start with the origin of very name 'Trinidad'. Did it come about because of three mountain peaks? Where, indeed, are the 'Three Sisters' that school-children have been made so much aware of during all the years?

Most important too is Columbus' image in the Americas, and indeed in the world. Was the 'Admiral of the Ocean Sea' as pious and saintly as popular stories would have us believe? How in fact did he and his few followers achieve his penetration into a 'New World' bristling with hostile warriors? Under ordinary circumstances would he and his company have survived? And what were the true motives for his being here in the first place? How did he carry out his explorations, what did he do, what did he meet, and how did he deal with this question of justice – especially in Haiti? And a very important question: when he arrived in these waters did he *really* think he was in India?

After five hundred years it is high time we looked into this slice of history, for Columbus' work was far too significant to merit just a passing glance.

The term 'Columbus discovered' is not used very much in this book, because, although Columbus (and by extension, Europe) did discover that these lands were there, the term in the historical and social context is far from being innocent and rather suggests that the lands became important only when Europe visited. For instance, Trinidadian children have had to read that Sir Walter Raleigh discovered the Pitch Lake. One can retort: 'Oh yes? Did Raleigh get there before the native peoples?' And wasn't the Pacific seen and known before Balboa 'discovered' it? Now is the time for the people of the world (and especially the Americas) to wipe out the needless bias in its history.

In reference to Haiti, which played a central part in all these voyages, the original name 'Haiti' is used constantly, and not Columbus' name for the island, which was 'Española'. In today's situation where Haiti is just a part of that island (the Dominican Republic being the other) it would be necessary to use Columbus' word for convenience sake, but since at the time the whole island was Haiti, and especially as 'Haiti' was the name its people gave to it, maybe it is better for us to let this name take pride of place.

Finally, since Columbus does not belong just to the Americas, nor to Spain, nor to Genoa, but in fact belongs to the world, it is for all readers that this book is written. And it is written to mark the 500th anniversary of the meeting of this great explorer with a great continent.

Michael Anthony,
Port-of-Spain.
1992

Introduction

There is no figure in the entire history of exploration who
has had such an impact on the world as Christopher Columbus.

Fig. 1   Christopher Columbus – a copy made by Attissime about 1555 of
an earlier portrait and therefore considered the oldest authentic portrait

The fact of Columbus' encounter in 1492 with the continent we now call America has had such a profound effect on history and on the mass movement of mankind that the matter hardly needs to be stressed. This is not to say that had Columbus not come upon the so-called 'New World' nobody else would have done it, and one is certainly not suggesting that Columbus set out to accomplish this, nor even when the deed was accomplished that he knew what he had done.

Another important thing to be said here and which might not be to the glory of Columbus is that the contact of this brave mariner with a world hitherto unknown to Europe heralded the beginning of a long, bitter age of conflict, colonialism, and slavery, of blood, sweat, and tears; an age typified by greed and graft, by unspeakable cruelty, by the lust for gold, as well as by falsehood, hypocrisy, and the destruction of innocence.

Yet on the whole what fascinates is the fact that considering the millions of years of the existence of the Earth, it was only in AD 1492 that people from one major part of this planet came to the realisation that the other part existed. The task here is not to look at what resulted from this knowledge, nor to trace the episodes of conquest and settlement which followed the arrival of Columbus in the 'New World'. The task is to look at the methods and motives, the skill, intuition, foresight, obsession, piety, and yes, craftiness, that made this great explorer reach and win a 'New World' for Spain. Of course, the terms 'New World' and 'Old World' are here used for convenience sake, for just as the term 'discovery by Columbus' might imply to some that the region was empty, lying awaste, or utterly unimportant before Columbus came, just so the term 'New World' might suggest it only became a world after the encounter by Columbus. Also, as far as geological time is concerned it is certainly as old as the 'Old World'.

Even Columbus' inaccurate term *'Indias Occidentales'* (West Indies) has become inconvenient, especially when historians keep using the term 'Indians' for the aboriginal peoples of America instead of the useful term 'Amerindians'. The term 'Indians' becomes even more ridiculous when used in relation to Trinidad or Guyana, where a large percentage of the population has its origin in the true India.

But it is interesting that 'The Indias', in Columbus' time, was a term loosely used to denote the easternmost parts of the world. For those who held that the Earth was a sphere, it was the first part one would come to if one was to sail west from Europe. Not many at the time knew of the landmass lying in the ocean between the Indias and the coasts of Europe and Africa.

However, all these thoughts pale into insignificance when we think of the great explorer. What was it that moved this remarkable man? The Spanish scholar, Salvador de Madariaga, alludes to the name Christopher, which means 'The Christ-bearer', and suggests that Columbus saw himself as the one chosen by God to take Christ (Christianity) to the 'heathen' world. De Madariaga also points to the coincidence of the name 'Colón', which was Columbus' surname in Spain, because the word also has a bearing on colonisation, which Columbus brought into the 'New World'. After 500 years the event of 1492 has become fascinating to us all, and we want to know exactly what transpired. For we remain in awe – almost disbelief – at the heroic story of Christopher Columbus. Perhaps it will not be amiss if we go into the details of the activities of this explorer.

Columbus, the Man

Cristoforo Colombo, called Christopher Columbus by the English, and Cristóbal Colón by the Spaniards, was born at Genoa, in Italy, in the year 1451. His father, Domenico, was a wool-weaver, and although some historians have stated that Columbus was of noble lineage, a matter subtly supported by his son, Ferdinand, this view is not encouraged by the records.

At the time that Columbus was born Genoa was one of the great trading centres of the Mediterranean and much commerce was carried on between this great city on Italy's Ligurian coast and places such as Alexandria in Egypt, Chios in Greece, the island of Cyprus to the east, and as far west as Ceuta in Morocco. It was therefore not strange that the boy Christopher would be fascinated by sea life and not too surprising that at fourteen we already observe him riding the Mediterranean waves, skilled in the craft of the seafarer. It is recorded that he fought with Tunisian galleys, and he must have been considered not just a trader but a seaman who could look after himself. In 1476 he was attacked by French pirates off Cape St Vincent, (the southern tip of Portugal) and his ship was bound to the enemy's by grappling irons. Then fire broke out. Columbus had to jump overboard about ten miles from the Portuguese coast and, with the aid of an oar in the water and his great prowess in swimming, he managed to reach the shore.

Columbus remained in Portugal for many years, and married Felipa Moniz in Lisbon. Out of this marriage his son Diego was born in 1480. Felipa died in 1485. Columbus later left Portugal for Spain, where Ferdinand was born in 1488.

As a young seaman Columbus entertained a great dream: sailing to the Orient, to a land of splendour and riches. Was

Fig.2   Genoa, taken from Schedel's *Liber Chronicarum,* 1493

there any substance in this dream, and what was the origin of it? Long before Christopher Columbus was born two Venetian brothers, merchants, travelled as far east as Cathay (China), to the court of the great Kublai Khan, in a city called Peking. On one of these journeys one of the brothers took his seventeen-year-old son, Marco Polo. That journey began in 1271 and they reached the court of the great Khan in 1275. Kublai Khan was so impressed with the young Marco that he prevailed upon him to stay, and Marco Polo stayed at the court of this Mongol prince for twenty years.

After Marco Polo returned home to Venice, in 1295, he was in charge of a galley which fought the Genoese at the battle of Curzola. The Genoese captured Marco Polo and imprisoned him in Genoa, and during this imprisonment Marco Polo dictated to another captive wonderful stories of the riches and splendour of the East. He spoke of the magnificent court of the great Khan, with treasures everywhere: rubies, jade, emeralds, gold, and precious stones; and he spoke of the resplendent Cathay, and of Cypango (Japan).

These stories did not become widely known until printing was invented by Johannes Gutenburg around 1455. They were then published, and they made such an impact on Europe that all its maritime nations entertained hopes of establishing contact with these lands, the *maritime* nations, for by this time only the sea route was available. The route taken by the Polos was from Venice by sea to Baghdad and by sea again to Ormuz, then overland across Persia through Balkh, Yarkand, and Suchau, then across the Gobi Desert until they came to the court of Kublai Khan at Peking in Cathay.

However, by the time of Columbus the overland route was cut off by the Turks, and those who wished to reach the eastern lands had to dare the dangerous sea route around the horn of Africa, a dreaded cape then called the 'Cape of Storms'. The stories of Marco Polo lit up the mind of the boy Columbus, and although by 1477 he had already entertained dreams of reaching the Orient, the route in his mind was not the route around the 'Cape of Storms'. For, having applied himself to the sciences of geography, astronomy, geometry, and navigation – sciences that no ambitious seaman could ignore –

and always seeking the company of scientists and astronomers, map-makers, and experienced mariners, he was profoundly convinced that the Earth was round. And since it was round, why head for the perilous 'Cape of Storms' and sail east? If the Earth was round then by heading west one was bound to come to the East. Columbus was encouraged in his belief of the Earth's roundness by Paolo Toscanelli, a physician and amateur astronomer of Florence. Toscanelli went as far as sending him a chart of the route he must take, and after receiving an enthusiastic reply from Columbus, wrote: 'I perceive your grand and noble desire to sail from west to east by the route indicated on the map I sent you, a route which will appear still more plainly upon a sphere. I am much pleased to see that I have been well understood, and that the voyage has become not only possible but certain, fraught with honour and gain, and most lofty fame among Christians'. This made Columbus even more eager to sail the western seas. Not that he had not faced those seas before. To show that the five zones were navigable he wrote around this time: 'In the month of February, 1477, I sailed one hundred leagues beyond the Island of Thule, whose northern part is in latitude 73 degrees north, and not 63 degrees as some affirm; nor does it lie upon the meridian where Ptolemy says the West begins, but much farther west.' Thule was Iceland.

Columbus had also shown his flair for sailing by visiting the Cape Verde Islands and the African coast at Sierra Leone, and so now he began to seek sponsorship for an expedition to the Indias. But, as could be expected, not many looked with favour on his plan to sail west. There were other factors. He applied to the Portuguese king, Dom João II, but Dom João II, apparently not wishing to entrust such an important expedition to any but a Portuguese mariner, did not accept. In fact he clandestinely despatched an expedition to test Columbus' plan, which caused Columbus to angrily turn his back on Portugal. Then Columbus tried Henry VII of England, but Henry was nurturing another Genoese explorer, Giacomo Caboto (John Cabot) and did not wish to consider the request at the time. (He did when it was too late.) Columbus tried the Court of Castile when he left Portugal, being referred to Queen

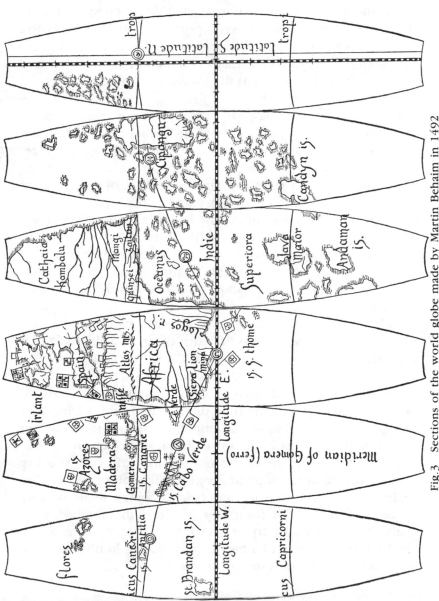

Fig.3 Sections of the world globe made by Martin Behaim in 1492

Isabella the Catholic, and although she did not immediately say 'Yes', he could not have failed to notice sympathy for his cause. In 1486 the Court of Castile gave him his first interview, and Bartholomew de las Casas reports: 'Their Majesties took note of his request, received it with gracious countenance, and decided to submit the matter to a committee of learned men . . . for at the moment they were very much concerned with the war'.

The war was the struggle to drive the Moors out of Spain.[1] The sovereigns of Spain, Ferdinand and Isabella, were spending huge sums in this endeavour and it would be another few years before they could even look at Columbus' plan. But in the meantime there was a setback. The 'committee of learned men' poured scorn on Columbus' plan and advised strongly against it. Whoever heard of going east by way of the west? Did Spain have money to waste on ships bound for the bottomless pit?[2] However, the sovereigns of Spain, especially Isabella, kept Columbus in mind. The struggle against the Moors went on relentlessly and on 2nd January 1492, Moorish resistance collapsed.

Did that, for Columbus, mean long-awaited success? Surprisingly the sovereigns of Spain came to a decision that what they called the 'Enterprise of the Indies' was over. The answer to Columbus was 'No'. Columbus packed his bags, saddled his mule, and with a heavy heart took the road to Cordova. But at the same time one of his faithful friends at the Spanish court, Luis de Santangel, went to find the queen and so shocked was he about Columbus' rejection that he prevailed upon her to reconsider. 'Think of what you are doing,' he told her, 'Think of the glory that might be awaiting Spain. Think of the gold and other riches which Spain so badly needs now. Think of the glory of God, the thousands of souls that are waiting to be saved . . .' Queen Isabella was deeply moved. She sent a messenger after Columbus and the messenger overtook him on the road.

1   The Moors had invaded Spain since the fifth century.
2   Those who felt that the Earth was flat thought ships would fall off the horizon into a bottomless pit.

Shortly afterwards Columbus and the king and queen of Spain began negotiations regarding the 'Enterprise of the Indies', and this resulted in the assignment to Columbus. There had never been such an assignment given to an explorer by the sovereigns of any country, and certainly no known mariner had undertaken to cross the western seas, at least at latitudes in the torrid zone. It is rather strange that in the Discovery Contract no mention was made of Columbus sailing for the Indias, and this has caused speculation that Columbus, having heard so many tales from mariners that there were islands in the western seas, did not particularly set off for India at all. There were no scarcity of tales of such lands and Dom João II, King of Portugal, had advanced the then famous theory that there was a land of gold and precious stones bestriding the Equator. And after all, had not the Norsemen, Eric the Red and Lief the Lucky, encountered Greenland, and gone further west to Vinland (New Foundland) and explored the coast of North America, as early as the tenth century? Many other stories of such exploits – some unknown to us – may have haunted Columbus.

This explorer, who is always presented as a rather naïve person, was very far from being naïve when he worked out the terms of the contract with the king and queen of Spain. Although he was anxious to undertake the voyage, he wanted to make sure that he received adequate reward and protection for himself and his family, not only for that period but for all times.

For example, the Discovery Contract begins by saying: 'Firstly, that Your Highnesses as actual Lords of the said Oceans, appoint from this date the said Don Cristóbal Colón to be your Admiral in all those islands and mainlands which by his activity and industry shall be discovered or acquired in the said oceans during his life-time, and likewise after his death, his heirs and successors one after another in perpetuity . . .'

Also, by the second article of the Contract, the admiral, having secured his appointment as Viceroy and Governor-General 'over all the said islands and mainlands he shall discover or acquire in the said seas', claimed the right to nominate three candidates for this office, from whom the sovereigns proposed to select one. Columbus further stipulated in the negotiations that he be given a tenth part of all and every kind of merchandise that he may come upon, 'whether pearls, precious stones, gold, silver, spices and other objects of merchandise whatsoever'. He also sought agreement that if he chose he may contribute an eighth part of the expenses of fitting out the ships, and that he be given an eighth part of the profits.

Yet for all this, the impression could easily be given that the principal reason for those four daring voyages of discovery was not greed or personal gain, but instead, deep religious concern. The Moors had overrun Jerusalem and this pious Catholic knew not a moment of peace. For example, here is an entry in his journal of the first voyage, written on Wednesday 26th December, 1492: 'I protested to Your Highnesses that all the profits of this my enterprise should be spent in the conquest of Jerusalem, and Your Highnesses laughed and said that it pleased them and that without this they entertained that desire . . . This undertaking is made with a view to expend what is derived from it in guarding the Holy Sepulchre for the Holy Church'.

And to Pope Alexander VI he wrote later: 'After I was there and had seen the land I wrote to the King and Queen, my Lords, that in seven years I would pay for 50,000 foot and 5,000 horse for the conquest of it, and in five more years 50,000 more foot and 5,000 more horse, making ten thousand horse and one hundred thousand foot – Satan has disturbed all this'. So we see that Columbus, among the many other sides to him, was what some may call a religious fanatic.

But what about Columbus the man of science and the mathematician? Although the scientists and mathematicians of the day might never have claimed him as their own, he delved into both these subjects, including astronomy – anything in fact to improve his skill in navigation. In order to carry out his voyage, Columbus, basing his calculations on what he accepted as the size of the Earth, and therefore the distance to be travelled, and after considering the course he would take, and the normal speed, worked out what he saw as the duration of the journey, and made preparations to suit. These calculations were based principally on the findings of Ptolemy (Claudius Ptolemaeus c. AD 90 – 168) the Egyptian geographer and astronomer whose work dominated his own period and right up to the seventeenth century. Columbus also consulted the calculations of Marinus of Tyre.

It turned out that the Earth was much larger than both Ptolemy and Marinus had estimated and in fact the true distance to India was more than twice as great as Columbus had allowed for. Yet coincidentally, the Genoese saw land just at the time he thought he should be arriving in the Orient. Had the great landmass we now call America not lain between, could we say what would have befallen the 'Admiral of the Ocean Sea'?

However, let us begin the story at the point where Columbus was at the Court of Spain with a Discovery Contract and ready to pursue the 'Enterprise of the Indies'. He certainly looked the part of a likely hero, for he was a tall, athletically-built man, neither 'fat or lean', as his son Ferdinand described him. He was now forty-one years old, and physically in possession of all his powers. From the age of thirty his hair had turned completely white, although he later told the sovereigns of Spain that it went white because of his labours in their service! He had an aquiline nose and eagle eyes, eyes which seemed to reflect the fire of his determination. And now he was about to embark.

For Spain and for others concerned the 'Enterprise of the Indies' was nothing but a golden quest.

CHAPTER ONE
The First Voyage

To Cross Uncharted Waters

After the signing of the agreement between Christopher Columbus and the sovereigns of Spain, on 17th April, 1492, there was the question of the sovereigns, Ferdinand and Isabella, providing the mariner with ships, fitting out those ships for the long voyage, and moreover, finding a crew for the ships. Finding a crew looked like being the most difficult task of all, for few people wished to dare those unknown seas lying to the westward. To say the least it seemed a terrifying prospect. For although the theory that the Earth was round had been advanced several centuries before, there were few that believed it up to Columbus' time. And no wonder, for it had never been put to the test, so far as was known. And in any case, how could the Earth be round when everyone was seeing it flat? And was it not madness to think that one could reach lands of the East by sailing west? Maybe some of the thinking men of the time could ponder the question and see if such a possibility existed. But it was not thinking men who were going to make up the crew for Columbus' voyage. It was hard, sturdy, coarse, labouring men, men who were physically able to stand up to the rigours of what was bound to be a long perilous journey, and men who were filled with bravado and able to stare danger in the face.

So the sovereigns, after learning of Columbus' difficulty (and their own) in getting a crew for the expedition, decided to take a certain measure. Two weeks after the signing of the agreement they did what they thought to be the only practical thing. In a letter dated 30th April 1492, they addressed all the Royal Officials (of prisons) thus:

Fig.4   King Ferdinand of Spain, from the Columbus letter, 1493

Be it known that we are sending Christopher Columbus across the Ocean to undertake useful enterprises in our service, and in order to obtain the crew he needs in the three vessels for the voyage, it is necessary to promise safety to those persons for otherwise they would not want to go with him on the said voyage . . . And we hereby promise safety to each and every person who will go on the said vessels with the said Christopher Columbus . . . so that no harm nor evil and no injury will befall their property, nor any of their possessions, because of any misdemeanour they might have done or committed up to the date of this letter during the time of their voyage and the time spent there, including their return voyage home and two months afterwards. We therefore command each and every one of you in your place and jurisdictions, not to take account of any criminal cause regarding the persons who may go with the said Christopher Columbus on the said three vessels during the aforesaid time.

So it was in this way that a crew was obtained for the first voyage: by granting a pardon to criminals and other offenders.

The three vessels that the sovereigns had referred to were the *Santa Maria*, the *Pinta*, and the *Niña*. The *Santa Maria* was to be Columbus' flagship, the *Pinta* (or chick) was to be commanded by Martin Alonso Pinzón, and the *Niña* (or little girl) was to be under the command of Martin's brother, Vincente Yañez Pinzón.

Columbus says in his journal: 'I left the City of Granada on the 12th of May in the same year, 1492, being a Saturday, and came to the town of Palos, which is a seaport, where I equipped three vessels well suited for such service. I departed from that port well supplied with provisions and with many sailors, on the 3rd August 1492, being Friday, half an hour before sunrise, and took the route for the Canary Islands of Your Highnesses, which are in the said ocean, that I might thence take my course and sail until I should reach the Indias . . .'

On that Friday, 3rd August, 1492, great crowds thronged the seaport and amidst scenes of high emotion friends and relatives took leave of the seamen, whom they felt they might never see again. Columbus, who had been to church to hear mass and to seek divine protection for his voyage, bade a fond

Fig.5   Columbus leaving Palos, bidding farewell to
Isabella and Ferdinand

farewell to the king and queen of Spain, who had come to
see him leave, and so with the church bells tolling he sailed
away from Palos and took a course south-west-by-south,
bound for the Canary Islands. They took three days to get
there, and after taking in the final necessities he set his course
due west and bravely ventured into the 'Sea of Darkness'.

The admiral, for the purpose of not getting the men too
concerned, kept two separate logs: one for himself in which
he recorded the true distances travelled, and the other for the
crew. In this second one, which was exposed for all to see,
he inserted false distances giving the impression that they had
not travelled very far.

The voyage went along uneventfully, with just sky and the
wide ocean, and, as expected, after a few days out the men
began to get restive. For more than a month they travelled
without seeing any sign of land, and then suddenly, on Sunday
16th September they saw something which lifted their hearts.
It was green seaweed floating near their ship, and they became

Fig.6   Detail from an engraving of 1621 showing
Columbus' ships leaving Spain

excited because they knew land just had to be near. The next
day they saw even more seaweed and other signs which told
them that journey's end was not too far away. For example,
examining the seaweed the seamen found a crab, and that

morning Columbus had seen a white bird. Everybody sailed on in high spirits.

Signs of land from now on were becoming so common that the sailors were hardly taking notice. Everyone was anxious to reach land. Rain fell, without any wind, and Columbus told his crew that this was another sign that land was near. He himself, the admiral, did not seem to decide on how to set his course. Sometimes he set it to the north-west, and sometimes to the south-west, and at times he sailed due west. He said he did this because he felt certain there were islands to the north and south of where he was. He sailed on and on, mainly keeping due west, and with now and then a calm, and now and then a full force of wind filling the sails. On average he was doing 50 miles a day. Now he kept due west, between the supposed islands, and he wrote in his log: 'And there is time enough, for God willing, on the return voyage all will be seen'.

However, despite all the signs of land they were seeing there was no landfall, and now, being about two months at sea, the sailors again became restive and uneasy. On one occasion birds made them feel that land was certainly nearby. But once again their hopes were dashed. Neither that day, nor the next, nor the rest of the entire week produced anything more hopeful than seaweed, birds, reeds, and barnacles, and now the men on all three of the caravels kept pressing their captains to turn back. Matters reached a serious stage on Tuesday 9th October when on the *Santa Maria* those desperate and ill-tempered men confronted Columbus. Mutiny reared its head. They called on him to turn back forthwith. They said they were going no further.

Columbus pleaded with the men. They had come so far, about 450 leagues, were they prepared to turn back without seeing land? And it was a certainty that land could not now be far away. Where did those birds come from, for example? There must be land somewhere nearby, and not only near, but very, very near. How could they turn back now, while they were on the brink of a land of gold and riches? Would they turn their backs on the Indias and return to Spain in shame? 'Come on', he cried. He told them they were brave

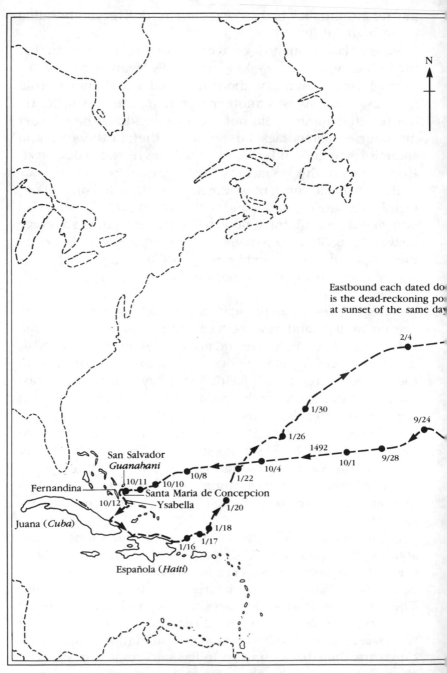

Fig.7   The course of Columbus' first voyage

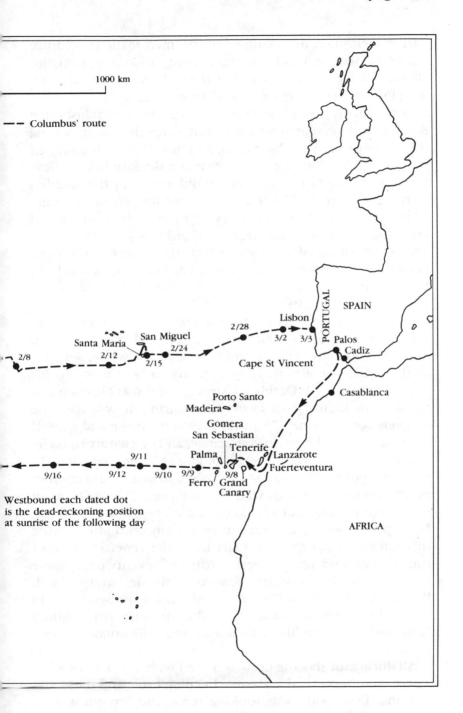

1000 km

– – Columbus' route

SPAIN

PORTUGAL

Lisbon
2/28
3/2   3/3   Palos
Cadiz

Santa Maria   San Miguel
2/12   2/24
2/8   2/15

Cape St Vincent

Casablanca

Porto Santo
Madeira

Gomera
San Sebastian

Palma   Tenerife
9/11
9/16   9/12   9/10   9/9   9/8   Lanzarote
Ferro   Grand   Fuerteventura
Canary

Westbound each dated dot
is the dead-reckoning position
at sunrise of the following day

AFRICA

daring men, men deserving of glory, men made to venture out and discover. Land was right there, beckoning to them. He said, 'Give me, my men, but three days'. If they did not see land in three days he would turn back.

With that promise the men agreed to go on, but for just three days! The ships ploughed the ocean, with the sailors seeing the usual seaweed and barnacles, and then there was a sudden delight. On Wednesday 10th October a flock of petrels flew towards the flagship. What message did they bring the 'Admiral of the Ocean Sea'? Was it a message of happiness to come, or of conflict, or fame and glory? To the excited, overjoyed crew there was only one message: land was just beyond the waves. The threat of mutiny was forgotten. The *Niña*, a faster vessel than Columbus' *Santa Maria*, began racing forward – in fact all three vessels went as fast as they could, each crew anxious to be the first to spot land.

Those in the caravels *Pinta* and *Niña* saw green reeds and barnacles, and green branches of trees, and they knew the moment had come – the moment when they would set foot in the Indias, or was it, in fact, going to be a new world?

On Thurday 11th October a strong wind was blowing and the sea rose higher than at any time during the voyage. The caravels accomplished 78 miles between sunrise and sunset. Now signs of land were in abundance, and of a nature to really cheer up the men. The *Niña* picked up another green branch, the *Pinta* got a cane and a stick, a piece of board, and another piece of wood that appeared to have been carved. Now all eyes were looking out for land, and all hearts were racing. For, apart from the excitement of finding land after daring this unknown ocean, and apart from the relief in store of touching ground again after a journey of seventy days, there was the added incentive of a reward for the first to sight land. Before they left Spain Queen Isabella had promised the sum of 10,000 maravedis annually to the first man who sighted land, and Columbus himself was offering a silk doublet to that person.

All during the day the crew watched with eyes like hawks'. There were several false alarms. Evening came and there was nothing. Everybody was looking tense and few must have spoken to each other. Then at ten o'clock there was drama. Columbus, standing at the back of the *Santa Maria*, thought he saw a light, but he was timid to cry out for, Las Casas says, it was 'so uncertain a thing that he did not wish to declare that it was land'. Columbus summoned Pedro Gutiérrez, who thought he saw it too, but another sailor Rodrigo Sanchez, said he saw nothing. There is very little doubt that the light the admiral saw was the light of his dreams and of his excited nature at that time. Samuel Eliot Morison, in his book, *Admiral of the Ocean Sea*, says: 'There is no need to criticise Columbus' seamanship because he sighted an imaginary light; but it is not easy to defend the fact that for this false landfall, which he must have known the next day to have been imaginary, he demanded and obtained the annuity of 10,000 maravedis promised by the Sovereigns to the man who first sighted land'.

However, the great moment was not long in coming. It was two o'clock the next morning – the morning of 12th October, 1492 – when Rodrigo de Triana saw something like a white cliff gleaming in the moonlight. He tore the air with his cry: 'Tierra! Tierra!' and this time it really was land. His captain, Martin Alonso Pinzón, came and verified it was land, then, according to the signal they had previously agreed upon, he fired a cannon into the air.

It is not possible to describe the jubilation which broke out on board the three caravels. There were singing and dancing, tears and prayers. Sails were shortened as the sailors moved to the land in the distance, their voices echoing the *Salve Regina* and the salt of the tears of joy joining the salt of the sea. The land, by Columbus' reckoning, was 6 miles away. Now they were merely awaiting daylight as they drifted into a new world.

Columbus Meets the 'New World'

The 'Admiral of the Ocean Sea', together with the crew of the *Santa Maria*, and along with the captains and the crew of the other two ships, stood and watched the natives of this the first place they had come to in the 'Indias'. On the other hand crowds of people stood on the shore gazing at the strange apparition in the waters before them. It was the first time they had seen such wondrous things. Before them there were three huge canoes on the water, with tall poles and sheets above them, but perhaps the most astonishing thing of all was the people in them. This was a tribe with white skins, and their bodies were covered, showing only their faces and their hands. Who were these people and what did they want? What was the land they came from?

Everyone came to the beach to see: the cacique, the warriors, the old men, all the women and the children. All the people of this island, Guanahani, came to gaze at something

Fig.8   Columbus landing, from a 15th-century book. Note the figure of King Ferdinand seated in the foreground

they had never dreamed of before, a strange tribe which appeared from over the water.

In the dawn the strange people left their huge canoes and came to shore in small ones, and as they arrived on the beach the natives fled. The first thing that Columbus did on arriving on land was to fall on his knees and thank God for bringing him safely to the 'Indias', and if there were natives courageous enough to stay by they would have been the first to hear one of the languages from the other world. Then Columbus and his men erected a cross with the letters 'F' and 'Y' for Ferdinand and Ysabella, and naming the island 'San Salvador' in dedication to the Holy Saviour, Columbus took possession of their island for Spain.

Of course the inhabitants of Guanahani knew nothing of what was going on. Later, they returned, and convinced that the strange tribe meant no harm, they gave their friendship.

But let us think of the impressions gained by either side. The natives of Guanahani did not have the art of writing, so what they felt remains lost forever, but not so the impressions of the 'tribe from the sunrise'. As soon as their 'chief', Christopher Columbus, went back to his cabin, he wrote in his journal for the benefit of his 'caciques', the king and queen of Spain: 'I knew they were a people to be delivered and converted to our holy faith rather by love than by force. I gave to some among them some red caps and some glass beads, which they hung around their necks, and many other things of little value. At this they were greatly pleased and became so entirely our friends that it was a wonder to see.'

This reaction might seem surprising to those who really believe that Columbus thought he was in the resplendent East, the land of riches that Marco Polo had written about. For it would seem that Columbus did expect to find a backward people, a people who were easily pleased; had he not brought red caps and glass beads with him? In his journal he spoke of these people as 'deficient in everything'. But he was impressed with their physical appearance, for in his journal we read: 'They were very well built, with very handsome bodies, and very good faces. Their hair is coarse, almost like the hair of a horse's tail, and short; they wear their hair down

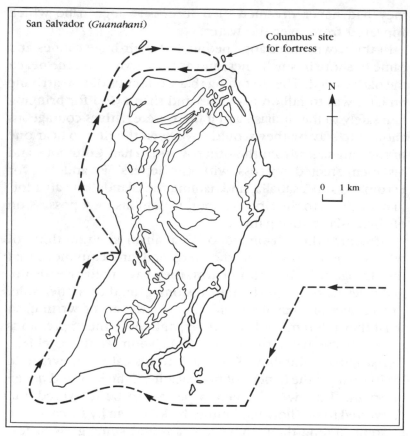

Fig.9   San Salvador, Columbus' first landfall

over their eyebrows, except for a few strands behind, which they wear long and never cut. Some of them are painted black and they are the colour of the people of the Canaries, and some of them are painted white, and some red, and some in any colour that they find ... They do not bear arms, nor know them, for I showed them swords and they took them by the blade and cut themselves through ignorance.'

Then Columbus, foreshadowing the slavery that was to befall these simple, innocent people, said: 'They should be good servants and of quick intelligence, since I see that they very soon say all that is said to them, and I believe that they would easily be made Christians, for it appeared to me that they had no creed. Our Lord willing, at the time of my departure I shall bring back six of them to Your Highnesses, that they may learn to talk'.

So the 'Admiral of the Ocean Sea' and his men, brought, with their first contact, the feeling of complete dominance, ownership, and superiority over all that lay in their path. The fact that Columbus planned to take six back to Spain 'that they might learn to talk', makes it clear that, for him, unless they spoke his language they could not speak.

Whatever the points of view that may arise, it was quite certain what was Columbus' quest. It was gold. There was not the least doubt about that. For in his entry for Saturday 13th October 1492, the very day after he arrived at Guanahani, he wrote in his log: 'They brought balls of spun cotton and parrots and spears, and other trifles, which it would be tedious to write down, and they gave all for anything that was given to them. And I was attentive and laboured to know if they had gold, and I saw that some of them had a small piece hanging from a hole which they have in the nose, and from signs I was able to understand that going to the south or going round the island to the south there was a king who had large vessels of it, and possessed much gold.'

As was seen, this was only his second day in what was to him a new world, but if the natives were already fed up with his persistent enquiries about gold, and wanted to get rid of him, then perhaps this was the best way to do it: speak of a land some distance away where there was a king who had much gold. But was there not indeed such a land?

Anyway Columbus and his men set sail in the afternoon of the next day, with the admiral stating quite clearly that the journey was to seek the gold that he had been told about. He now writes something in his log which makes us feel sure that he really thought he was in the replendent East. For he states: 'I wish to go and see if I can make the Island of Cypango.' Cypango was an early name for Japan.

Before Columbus set out to find this king who had much gold, he threw light on a puzzling question. For one could well ask how it was that a people, said to be warlike, welcomed the Spaniards instead of opposing them. Columbus, in his log, told the king and queen of Spain that after preparing the ships to leave he went to see the other side of the island. He wrote: 'They ran towards us and we understood they were asking us if we came from Heaven.'

Of course the Spaniards told them yes, that was exactly where they came from, and it also appears that the Spaniards gave the impression that as Gods, they could not die. This was something that the natives were soon to put to the test.

It must be said, though, that from the first moment of their arrival in this 'New World' the Spaniards never acted as though they came from heaven. Even the humble and pious Columbus who thanked God at every moment for His protection and guidance, and for leading him to these people, never truly looked upon the natives as brothers – in other words, as God's children. True, he might not have looked upon them as beasts to be driven and exploited, as some of the desperate men in his company proved to do, but there is no question but that he saw them as inferior beings, and he showed this by his very first act of claiming their islands for Spain. It was obvious that he felt that Europe had a God-given right to all their possessions.

Addressing Ferdinand and Isabella in his log and recounting how that day the natives of the island called to him and wanted him to land, he said: 'But I feared to do so, seeing a great reef which encircled the whole island . . . It is true that inside the reef there are some shoals, but the sea is no more disturbed than the water in a well. And to see all this I went that morning in order to give an account of all to Your Highnesses and also to say where a fort should be built.'

He saw a suitable piece of land which he said could be converted into a fort in two days. He continued: 'Although I do not see that it is necessary to do so, for these people are very unskilled in arms, as Your Highnesses will see from the seven I have caused to be taken in order to carry them off that they may learn our language and return.'

Columbus then says: 'However, when Your Highnesses so command they can all be carried off to Castile, or held captive in the island itself, since with fifty men they would be all kept in subjection, and forced to do whatever may be wished.'

Anyway, Columbus hoisted sail from Guanahani on Monday

15th October in that year 1492, and the objective was to find the island where lived this king who had much gold. The tide swelled against him but he pressed on. He reached an island which he named 'Santa Maria de Concepcion', today's Rum Cay, and in his log that night he gave a brief description to the sovereigns of Spain of the two islands he had seen so far – the newly-named San Salvador and Santa Maria de Concepcion – saying that he would have liked to look at them better so as to describe them more fully, but, he wrote, 'I do not wish to delay in finding gold.'

The people on Santa Maria de Concepcion told him it was true there was an island nearby where people wore big bracelets of gold on both arms and legs, and there were gold rings hanging from their ears and noses, and there were gold chains around their necks. In his log Columbus points out to Ferdinand and Isabella that this must be so because these people knew gold, adding, 'Because I showed them some pieces of gold which I have. I cannot fail, with the aid of the Lord, to find the place whence it comes.'

As a result, Columbus spent the next few days hunting the elusive gold-rich isle, going from place to place and renaming each island as he went. With Santa Maria de Concepcion behind him he met one which he named 'Fernandina' (after King Ferdinand) and the next one he saw he called 'Ysabella' after his beloved queen. (Fernandina is now called Long Island and Ysabella, Crooked Island.) These were just two of the many islands in the group now called the Bahamas.

As to the gold, although the natives he had caused to be taken on Guanahani told him of people wearing this metal on their arms and legs, when he reached the supposed island he saw no such thing. He wrote in his log: 'I can well believe that all they said was a ruse to get away.'

But Columbus' mind was now even more lit up with gold, because although he did not see the very large gold bracelets he had been told about, nevertheless he did see people wearing pieces of gold and he was determined to get as much of it as he could.

These were still the early days of navigational instruments, and Columbus, using a mariner's astrolabe as well as the naked

Fig. 10   A 16th-century mariner's astrolabe

eye, was not always accurate. There were cases when he
confused the sizes of the islands he met. He also described
the houses as having fine chimneys, but this was not a mistake.
This was just one of the many attempts of Columbus to mis-
lead the sovereigns of Spain, and for a reason we shall see
presently. The houses had no chimneys at all, just holes to
let the smoke out. Also in this vein he praised the landscape

out of all proportion to reality.

It must be borne in mind that Columbus was not as naïve as he is often presented. He knew the opposition that Isabella had faced to get him off on the expedition, and he knew that the sovereigns had spent a great deal of money to hire the vessels, fit them out, find crew and other officials, and to finally despatch him on this great journey. And he was conscious of the high hopes entertained. So now he was bent on telling them astonishing things to keep them cheered up and excited. Therefore he embellished upon almost every single thing. A good example of this was his writing in his log of an occasion when, on the island he called Fernandina, he waited a long while for some of his men who had gone in search of water. He wrote: 'During this time I walked amongst trees and they were the loveliest sight I have yet seen. They seemed to be as green as those of Andalusia in the month of May, and all the trees are as different from ours as day is from night, and so is the fruit, and the stones and the grasses, and everything else. I saw many trees very unlike ours; and many of them had many branches of different kinds, and all coming from one root. One branch is of one kind and another branch is of a different kind, and they are so unlike each other that it is the greatest wonder in the world.'

Other descriptions sound factual though exaggerated. Continuing the same letter the admiral wrote: 'There are fish so unlike ours that it is a marvel. There are some shaped like dories and of the finest colours in the world: blue, yellow, red, and of all colours, and others painted in a thousand ways, and the colours are so fine that no man would not wonder at them or be anything but delighted to see them. There are also whales. I saw no land animals of any kind, except parrots and lizards. A boy told me that he saw a large snake. I did not see any sheep or goats or other animals, but I have been here a very short while and it is now midday.'

And indeed he had been there only a short while, for the day was Tuesday 16th October 1492, just four days after he had arrived in the 'Indias'. There was in fact little animal life on those islands he had explored. The only sheep and goats that were to appear there were the sheep and goats the

Spaniards were to take there themselves.

Columbus did not tire of writing letters to Ferdinand and Isabella, telling of 'wondrous' things to be seen in these lands, but the most wondrous thing he wanted to be able to tell the sovereigns was that he had found gold. This continued to obsess him and his men. He was a little bewildered now as to where gold was actually to be found for he was beginning to get the impression that the people who pretended to direct him to gold were making a fool of him. Also, he was growing more and more worried by the behaviour of some of his men, whose greed for gold and the desire to return rich to Spain were making them overbearing. It rained that evening of 16th October, and Columbus, anxious to set out but apprehensive that the mist would make it more difficult to navigate, complained: 'So it has rained more or less every day since I have been in these Indias.'

Nevertheless the admiral set out, using his eyes and ears, anxious to steer in the direction of gold. Just about this time a guide told him of another king who wore a great deal of this precious metal, and that night he wrote in his log: 'Tomorrow I wish to go far inland to find this village and to see or have speech with this king.' The next day he set sail for the island and came to a cape, which he called 'Cabo del Isleo', the north-western point of what today is Crooked Island. He went ashore, but he saw no village there, just a single house from which all the occupants had fled in terror. They left all their household goods behind but Columbus said he ordered his men to touch nothing. This island cast a spell on Columbus and he felt its enchantment. That night he wrote in his log: 'The singing of the little birds is such that it seems a man could never wish to leave this place. The flocks of parrots darken the sun, and there are large and small birds of so many different kinds . . . '

But the scene was not so poetic when they met a snake, which his men pursued and killed – the first blood the Spaniards drew in their 'New World'. They were to draw a great deal more.

Columbus did not stay long anywhere for it was gold that was lighting up his mind and he wanted to get on his way.

He collected a number of things to take back to his ship including the snake's skin and a plant he deemed to be aloes, and he left for the village in question. At last they came to the village, but the people all fled when they saw the strange sight of bearded white-faced men, with their bodies sheathed from neck to toe, and with the hands holding shields and swords instead of bows and arrows. They fled in confusion and the Spaniards simply took the water they required and went back to their ships. But Columbus had not forgotten the king he was trying to find and now he was told that the village with this king lay much farther on. The admiral wrote in his log: 'If the weather permits I shall presently set out to go round the island until I have had speech with this king and I can see whether I can obtain from him the gold which I hear that he wears.'

As could be imagined, by that time the inhabitants had already told Columbus a great deal about the nature of the islands and a number of stories as to where gold was to be found. Most of those stories were fanciful, for as could well be guessed, many of them were given at the point of the sword, and others in a desire to see the Spaniards on their way. However, the quest was for gold, and now, although Columbus did not know it, he was about to set off for what was destined to be his most memorable interlude of the voyage.

After telling the Spanish sovereigns of his plans to visit the rich king, he declared: 'Following this I wish to leave for another very large island, which I believe must be Cypango, according to the signs these Indians who I have with me make. They call it Colba. They say that there are ships and very good sailors there. Beyond this island there is another which they call Bohio, which they say is also very large.'

As has been said earlier, Columbus' reference to Cypango certainly confirms that he believed that he was in the East and near India, for it will be remembered that Cypango was Japan. When Columbus said the people called it 'Colba' it was a slight mistake on his part, for what they called the island was 'Cuba'. Bohio was a nearby island which most of the inhabitants called 'Haiti'. Columbus headed for Cuba first, but it was Haiti which beckoned – a land he was to explore more than any other, and a land that he could not forget, nor could its people forget him.

Columbus in 'Española'

It was already 28th October when Columbus sailed into Cuba, the country he said he believed was Cypango or Japan. The previous morning he had left a little group of islands he had called 'Las Islas de Arena', or 'Islands of Sand', because it was very shallow off those islands, and he could see the sand at the bottom for about 20 miles. He travelled about 70 miles that day, heading south-south-west, and at nightfall the coast of Cuba rose to them amidst a heavy shower of rain. Because of the fear of reefs they waited offshore, and the next morning, Sunday 28th October, he entered what he called a lovely river, with the water crystal clear and free from shoals, and with as many as 12 fathoms depth at the river mouth. Describing the river Columbus said, 'All the neighbourhood of the river was full of trees, lovely and green, and different from ours, each one with flowers and fruit after its kind. There were many birds and small birds which sang very sweetly. There were a great number of palms, different from those of Guinea, and from ours. Their base had no bark and their leaves were very large. They cover their houses with them. The land is very flat. I have never witnessed a scene so beautiful.'

Charmed, Columbus jumped into the boat and went ashore. He saw two houses, which were obviously the homes of fishermen for he saw nets of palm fibre, lines and fish-hooks made of bone. Of course the Spaniards ransacked the houses. There was nobody around; the occupants, seeing the Spaniards, had fled in terror.

Columbus called the harbour 'Mares' and described it as one of the best in the world. He said there was a point where there was a rocky hillock and at that point it would be good to establish a fort.

Earlier that day he had sent two of his men, Rodrigo Sanchez and a boy called Diego into the forests to search for mastic trees, which were medicinal, and to see what else they found, and the next day the men returned with stories the admiral was eager to hear. They had gone about 40 miles, they said, as far as a village of about fifty houses, and about one thousand inhabitants. They said the houses were like tents, and that they were lodged in the best ones, being received with great solemnity, with men and women and children coming to look upon them. They told the admiral: 'These people touched us and kissed our hands and feet wondering at us and believing that we came from Heaven, and so we gave them to understand.'

This was great news for Columbus, the Spaniards being looked upon in every part as having come from heaven. For this meant that no harm would come to them. Yet it could not have taken long for the Spaniards to prove that they had come from elsewhere. The two men who had gone into the forests could not have done much damage, as they were only two, but soon droves of them began finding their way to the interior to impose on good nature and to harass the villagers for gold – as if gold was the only thing of value that heaven recognised.

From that day when they first arrived in Cuba – 28th October – the Spaniards spent their time roaming the countryside in the vicinity of the river, looking for inhabitants, most of whom fled on seeing them; entering villages, seizing whoever they could, searching, enquiring, looking for any signs of gold.

After a little stay at the harbour of Mares, Columbus moved further eastward, still with the quest for gold, and searching for the court of the Great Khan. He went from harbour to harbour, bay to bay, admiring the beauty of the countryside, marvelling at the simplicity and gentleness of the people, and writing to the sovereigns of Spain about the marvellous things he was seeing and hearing day by day. He was proceeding south-east towards the eastern end of Cuba.

Although up to this time, well into November, he had not got anything of value, he was extremely impressed with the land and people of Cuba, and on the night of 27th November he wrote in his log: 'How great will be the benefit which can be derived from this land I do not write. It is certain, Sovereign

Princes, that where there are such lands there must be many things of value. But I do not delay in any harbour because I wish to see as many lands as I can in order to give an account of them to Your Highnesses. And moreover I do not know the language and the people of these lands do not understand me nor does anyone I have with me understand them. These Indians also who I carry with me I often misunderstand, taking one thing for the contrary, and I have no great confidence in them because several times they have tried to escape.' Now more than ever they were trying to escape, as Columbus continued down the south-east coast of Cuba, and the reason for this will be told presently.

Anyway, looking at his log entry again for 27th November, we see he told Ferdinand and Isabella that there would be no difficulty whatsoever in converting the inhabitants of Cuba to Christianity since they had no creed and did not worship any idols[1]: He then proceeded to tell them about the land, and wrote: 'I certify to Your Highnesses that nowhere under the sun do I think can be found lands superior in fertility, in moderation of cold and heat, and in abundance of good and healthy water . . . For praise be to Our Lord up to the present among all my people I have not had one who has had a headache, or who has been in bed from illness, except one old man through pain from gravel, from which he has suffered all his life, and he was speedily well in two days. This, I say, is the case in all the three vessels.' Columbus was exaggerating here, for he himself had begun to suffer from arthritis.

Realising that Cuba had very little gold – at least in the part where he was – Columbus felt anxious to move on to Baneque, for this was the name of the island with the rich king. But he could not go to Baneque, for the wind upon him was north-east. Anyway, he decided to take advantage of the north-easterly wind and leave Cuba, which, because of its extent, he thought of as the mainland, for he had gone 400 miles along one side of it. The day that he left Cuba was Wednesday 5th

---

1   Little is known about the religion of the Arawaks. Columbus' men and later Spaniards were too busy converting the 'heathens' to observe their creed.

December. He called the point he sailed from 'Cabo Alpha y Omega'[2], Cape Maisi today. He also renamed the land of Cuba, 'Juana'.

He went further east, into the passage which divided Cuba from the other big island, Bohio, and this was the reason why his guides were trying to escape. For it meant that they were getting near to the island of Bohio, or Haiti, an island where lived a tribe, they said, who fed on human flesh. They had begged Columbus not to take them to Bohio, but Columbus had ignored them, suspecting that the people of Bohio were people of the Grand Khan who, being more intelligent than these timid people, captured them as slaves.

Columbus crossed the passage, and that night, still sailing east, and keeping to the north of the coast of Haiti, or Bohio, he saw a small island, and while passing between this small island and the large one he may have seen many turtles for he gave the island the name for turtle in Spanish – Tortuga.

The date was 6th December, and, being not many leagues from the shore of Haiti, he noticed a lovely harbour and sailed towards it. At first he named it 'Puerto Maria', but remembering that it was St Nicolas Day, he renamed the harbour 'Puerto de San Nicolas'. As he had crossed the passage from Cuba to Haiti, or Bohio, he had seen a number of fires lighting up the hills, and now on the morning of the following day he saw smoke. He did not know at that time that it was the native peoples who had been warning of his approach. Anyway the message could not have been completely effective for when he eventually entered Puerto de San Nicolas the people were taken by surprise and fled in terror.

Shortly before, the native guides he had with him, frantic and distressed at being brought to this island, again told Columbus the story. They were terrified and told ghastly tales of having been attacked by the man-eaters whose province was 'Caniba', and who were called Canibs or Caribs. At first the admiral did not believe them, feeling that they would try anything to get away. In the end, however, he was beginning to believe, and he entertained hopes of seizing at least one

2   Alpha y Omega, 'The first and the last'.

of these people to take back to Spain with him.

He was going to take back all sorts of things to Spain if only to confound his critics and prove that he had found a 'New World'. There were many scores of curiosities he was keeping on the ship, among them animals and plants and other objects, and most of all, he was hoping to take back, not curiosities, but a lot of gold. He headed for the coast ahead of him, and with the wind changing constantly. It was morning when he set out, and by sunset he had made some 88 miles. They drew close to the harbour he had called San Nicolas and he shortened his sails and waited for the dawn.

The day was Thursday 6th December, when Columbus entered Puerto de San Nicolas. He found it extremely beautiful, and with a magnificent-looking headland to the south-west

Fig.11   Columbus lands on Española (Haiti) and is greeted by Caribs, from an engraving by de Bry. It is interesting to note the Caribs portrayed giving European-style gifts to Columbus

which he called 'Cabo Estrela', or Cape Star. The next day he left Puerto de San Nicolas and as the sky showed signs of a storm he entered a more sheltered port, one he called 'Puerto de la Concepcion'.

He was extremely charmed by the countryside. From Puerto de la Concepcion he looked out upon lovely plains, and at once his mind wandered to the finest landscapes he had seen in Spain and decided that this was even better. As the land made him think about Spain so much he named it 'Española'[3]. After spending just a few days, receiving great courtesies from the people, watching the cultivated stretches of land, and the scenery that for him was so difficult to adequately describe, he wrote in his log, first speaking about the people: 'Your Highnesses should feel great joy, because they will presently become Christians, and will be educated in the good customs of our realm, for there cannot be a better people or country, and the number of the people and the extent of the country are so great that I no longer know how to describe them. For I have spoken in the superlative of the people and the land of Juana, which they call Cuba, but there is as great a difference between that and this as between night and day. Nor do I believe that anyone who has seen this would have done or said less than I have said and say. For it is true that the things here are a wonder, and the great peoples of this island of Española – for so I call it (and they call it Bohio) all display the most extraordinarily gentle behaviour, and have soft voices – unlike the others, who seem to threaten when they talk.'

After describing them as men and women of good height, Columbus goes on: 'It is true that they all paint themselves, some black, and others some other colour, and the majority red. (I have learnt that they do this on account of the sun so that it may not harm them so much.) The houses and villages are so lovely, and in all there is Government, with a judge or lord of them, and all obey him to the extent that it is a wonder. And all these lords are men of few words and excellent manners, and their method of giving orders is

---

3 'España' is Spain. 'Española' suggests 'Big Spain', since Columbus thought Haiti was bigger than Spain.

generally to make signs with the hand, and it is understood, so that it is a marvel.'

Columbus and his men sailed into a river in this harbour, and according to the admiral, the enchantment of this place was remarkable. The setting was extremely beautiful, he said, describing the river as flowing through plains and green fields. He took a net to fish, and according to him, before he reached the shore, a fish of a kind he had seen in Spain jumped into his boat. Columbus was delighted. It was the first time he had seen something exactly like what he had known in Spain. Except gold, of course: gold was the great exception, and he had seen a little copper. It was gold that he was always thinking of and this precious metal seemed to occupy his thoughts throughout his sleeping and waking hours. He now walked a little into the country, hoping to see someone to talk to so that he could ask about gold. On his way he found myrtle and other plants that in his opinion were exactly like those he had seen in Spain. He must have concluded that he could not have given this land a more apt name than Española. Before the Spaniards returned to the ships they saw five men, but unfortunately nothing could be asked of them for on seeing the Spaniards they all took flight.

It was here that the admiral came to realise that the fires he had seen were fires with which the people of the villages were warning each other of the approach of the Spaniards, and, in fact, at this stage the presence of the strange tribe must have been known throughout the islands and in various parts of the mainland. (Of course, the Spaniards did not yet know there was a mainland.)

It rained heavily while Columbus was at the port, and the weather was bad for two days, and while the admiral waited he again speculated on this place he called Española. He spoke of the great size of the island and said that he had the impression that it was bigger than Spain, but this was just another of Columbus' many mistakes. In any case he had only seen a little part of the north coast, so apart from what his guides had told him, he had no idea of the size. Spain, with 504,000 square kilometres, is nearly seven times as extensive as Haiti.

After the two days of bad weather Columbus found that he still could not leave Puerto de la Concepcion because of prevailing bad conditions. But he did not mind as he was most anxious, he said, to explore the strait between Tortuga and Española because his guides had told him it was in that direction he would find Baneque, the place of much gold. The guides also incorrectly told Columbus that Haiti (Española) was much larger than Cuba. They even went as far as to tell him that the island, Haiti, was not completely surrounded by water.

By that last assertion Columbus naturally felt that he had reached the continent, and therefore he was in the vicinity of the court of the Great Khan. This confirmed his belief that the people his guides feared were simply an intelligent race that dwelled in the region of the Great Khan. In respect to this Columbus wrote: 'And so I repeat what I have said on other occasions – that the Caniba tribe are nothing else than the people of the Grand Khan, who must be very near here and possess ships, and they probably come to take them as captives, and as prisoners do not return they believe that their captors eat them. Every day we understand these Indians better than they understand us, although many times there has been misunderstanding.'

The next day the weather was still not favourable and Columbus, unable to sail, got his men to construct a great cross. That day Columbus set up the cross at the entrance to the harbour, 'as a sign,' he wrote to the king and queen of Spain, 'that Your Highnesses hold this land as your own, and especially as an emblem of Jesus Christ, our Lord, and to the honour of Christendom.'

But could Christ have been a party to it? Columbus believed this to be the region of the Great Khan. Would he have been pleased if, just to reciprocate, the Great Khan had sent men to put up his symbol in Spain and claim Spain as his own? The pious and christian Columbus clearly did not subscribe to the words of Christ: 'Do unto others as you would have them do unto you.' Indeed, by this period, just a few weeks after the arrival of the Spaniards, the natives were already being violated, robbed, and ill-treated. How the admiral dealt with this, one is not sure, for he himself gives no details, but mentions the complaints of the caciques. However, we are sure of one thing: in Columbus' anxiety to obtain gold he stopped at nothing to have it wrested from the natives, even in the name of Christ. And quite calmly he was offering their land to the sovereigns of Spain to hold as their own.

While still in Puerto de la Concepcion the Spaniards captured a native woman and brought her to the ship, and Columbus had her treated well, clothed her, and sent her back to land again for the express purpose of having her go out and say that the Spaniards were good people. For Columbus was growing worried at the reputation that the Spaniards were getting. Everybody began fleeing on the sight of the Spaniards. The woman and the other natives Columbus had brought on the ship went out to the villages saying that the Spaniards were not like the Canibas, or Caribs, but in fact were good people who had come from heaven. This so impressed the villagers that they came to see the Spaniards and brought them many gifts, and even invited them to their homes. It was on visiting their homes that the Spaniards first saw *niamas*, the edible root that we know as yams today.

Bartholomew de las Casas, who came into possession of the Columbus papers, wrote: 'The Christians said that when at last the natives had lost their fear, they went to their houses, and each one of them brought what they had to eat, which is bread of niamas – that is, of roots like large carrots, which they grow, for they sow and grow and cultivate this in all these lands, and it is their mainstay of life.'

Las Casas, who was later called the 'Apostle of the Indians', and who sailed with Columbus on his third voyage of discovery, went on to declare, 'They make bread with these roots, and boil and roast them, and they taste like chestnuts, so that no one eating them would believe that they were anything but chestnuts'.

Incidentally, Las Casas, who became a priest, spent his life in fighting for these Arawak peoples, who fell prey to the brutality of the Spaniards. In fact, he it was who recommended that African slaves be imported to the 'Indias', because, from his point of view, they were hardy, and would ease the burden of the native peoples.

Curiously enough, neither Las Casas nor Columbus talked about the relationship of the Spaniards with the native women, but it is certain that the social order of things had already begun to be disrupted. For it will be remembered that these were men without women, having left their homes months before. Also, it will be borne in mind that these were bold uninhibited men, most of whom had been offenders of the law. Yet it appeared that at this point, and for a short while, there was growing a harmonious and beautiful relationship between the natives of these islands and the Spaniards, and this was certainly because the Spaniards were believed to have come from heaven.

The Spaniards returned to their ships, anxious to set sail, for as pleasant as their experiences at Puerto de la Concepcion were, they had as yet found no gold, neither had the letter to the Great Khan been delivered.

Before Columbus lifted anchor, he wanted to test the length of day and night in these parts for it seemed passing strange to him that the days were as long as the summer days in Spain, although it was December, when the days should be very much shorter than the nights. He passed sand through his hour glass and it told him that from sunrise to sunset it was ten and a half hours.

As soon as Columbus could sail he left the port of Puerto de la Concepcion and went across to explore the island of Tortuga, probably believing it to be Baneque. Tortuga was no Baneque.

Although Columbus wanted to press forward, he did so very reluctantly, and even on 16th December, ten days since he had landed in Haiti, he was still in the western part of the island, between Puerto de la Concepcion and Tortuga. Indeed, he was basking in a warm relationship with the people, and that day, 16th December, a cacique, with a retinue of 500 men, came to see him. That night, in a letter to the sovereigns of Spain he described the people as the best people in the world. Undoubtedly on the instigation of Columbus one of the natives who had been with the Spaniards went to this cacique or king when he was alone and told him that the Spaniards had come from heaven expressly in search of gold, and that they wanted to go to the island of Baneque and it would be well if that island had much gold. The king then described the route to the island of Baneque, and he added that if there was anything in his kingdom that the Spaniards desired, he would be only too happy to give it.

In his letter, Columbus described the place as beautiful beyond words and he said that the people were the loveliest he had seen. He told the sovereigns that the king as well as his subjects were going about 'as naked as their mothers bore them,' and that they were strong and robust. He said he told the king he was sent by Ferdinand and Isabella of Spain, and to the other Spaniards this must have been a slip of the tongue. Anyway, neither the king nor his subjects believed a word of it. They insisted that the Spaniards had come from heaven, and no doubt concluded that if they had come from Spain at all, then Spain was in heaven. It was certainly not in this world. Columbus, exploiting the innocence and the good nature of these people proved that he had nothing to do with heaven when in another letter to Ferdinand and Isabella, he said: 'Your Highnesses may believe that these lands are of such extent, good and fertile, and especially those of this island of Española, that no one knows how to describe them, and no one can believe it unless he has seen it. And you may believe that this island and all the others are as much your own as Castile, so that there is lacking here nothing except a settlement, and then to command the people to do what you wish. For I, with these people whom I carry with me, who are not many, could go about all these islands without meeting opposition, for I have seen three of these sailors land alone where there was a crowd of Indians and they all fled.'

In another part he said: 'They have no arms, and are all naked, and without any knowledge of war, and very cowardly, so that a thousand of them would not face three. And they are also fitted to be ruled and to be set to work, to cultivate the land and to do all else that is necessary, and you may build towns and teach them to go clothed and adopt our customs.'

The following night was another significant night. That was the night of Monday 17th December 1492, and Columbus was in the little village where he had first met the king. Today the

place is called Port de la Paix – Port of Peace – and there was
ample peace there on that occasion. But also on that occasion
the Spaniards saw signs of aggression against these people by
other tribes. The villagers showed Columbus some Carib
arrows, with which they had been assailed, and these were
the proof that these Caribs or Canibas existed. The arrows
were very much larger than the normal ones, fire-hardened,
and sharp. Two of the men showed Columbus huge cavities
on their buttocks, and they said that the Canibals had bitten
mouthfuls from them. Columbus felt he could not believe
this.

From the ship he sent some men into the village to see what
gold they could get and they managed to get a small quantity
of the metal which was worked into a thin leaf. It was as a
result of this that Columbus went into the village and met a
man whom he took to be the Governor but whom they called
'cacique'. Apparently it was the first time he had heard that
word. The cacique had another gold leaf, this one as large as
his hand, and he broke it into pieces and he exchanged it with
Columbus for glass beads and other trifles. When the pieces
were finished he said he would send for more the next day.
It was not surprising therefore that Columbus should comment
thus: 'These people are more alert and intelligent than all those
I have found up to this time.'

It was nearing Christmas in that year 1492, and Columbus
had been more than two months in this 'New World'. He did
not want to tarry much longer – in fact he was eager to get
back to Spain to tell of his wondrous discoveries, to set the
'Old World' agog with amazement, to let Spain's enemies burn
with jealousy, and of course to show the dear and beloved
Queen Isabella that all the trouble she took to get Spain to
sponsor the voyage – all her years of support for him at the
Court of Spain, amidst the laughter of their detractors – were
richly justified. None had believed he could reach the Indias
by sailing west, nor even survive by going into that unknown
'Sea of Darkness'. But he had done so and had discovered new
territories for Spain. His heart beat fast, and he felt anxious
to get across the seas again to excite Spain and bask in a shower
of glory. But he would not tarry in Spain for there was a lot

to do in these new lands. In fact the main thing was not done yet – that was to find gold. He knew there was gold and in fact he had not even been to Baneque yet. He was anxious to leave and to be at the Court of Spain to report on the Indias, and to return in haste. He would return with a bigger company of crew and settlers so that there would be no problem in subduing any who should think of opposing the Spaniards, and at the same time there would be enough people to found a settlement for Spain in these parts. He was also glad to return because he had faithfully kept a diary of all his experiences on this voyage, as well as the fact that he had written several letters to Ferdinand and Isabella, all of which letters of course were with him in his cabin, for he himself would have to take them back to Spain.

On 18th December an old man made the admiral's eyes light up with talk of abundant gold. The old man told him that just a few hundred miles away there were islands where gold was common-place, and that in fact one island itself seemed to be made of gold. Columbus became feverish with excitement. He asked the old man to take him and show him the place but the old man made a lot of excuses about why he could not go, and Columbus wanted to take him by force, but the old man happened to be a very important subject of the king of that place and Columbus did not want animosity. There would be time enough, he consoled himself. He left the huge cross in the harbour, and the next day, Wednesday 19th December, he set sail out of that channel that lies between Tortuga and Haiti.

On Thursday 20th December he saw a harbour and he was so struck by it that the next day he went in the ship's boat to get to its beach. He was embarrassed when later on in his cabin he wrote this entry in his log: 'I have praised so much the harbours that I have already visited, that I do not know how to praise this one, for fear it is thought that I am doing so excessively. I have spent 20 years at sea without coming off it for any length of time, and I have seen all the east and west; I have gone to England and to Guinea. But in all these parts I have not found the perfection of this harbour.'

Then he began to describe the harbour and the people

Fig.12   The three caravels at sea, from an engraving published in 1583

who came from the village nearby. Columbus said that at
first they had fear of the Spaniards, but after they had lost
their fear they came bringing bread, made of yams, and they
brought water in gourds[4], and in clay pitchers[5]. They also

4   Calabashes.
5   Goblets.

brought fruits, which the admiral found so wonderful that he preserved some to take back to Spain. It was a place of great enchantment for Columbus and he seemed to like it more than anywhere else he had been in these Indias, and in continuing to write about it in his log he repeated the same sentiments as before. He declared: 'I have spoken so well of other places, what shall I say of this?'

He had his mind so set on going to this 'Island of Gold' that the old man had told him about that on the Tuesday, which was Christmas Day, he left the harbour, which he called 'Santo Tomas'[6], and he thought he would just go and see it. As a result of his feeling exhausted, not having slept for two days and nights, he left the steering of his flagship to a young ship's boy. Placing the steering wheel in the hands of the ships' boys was something that Columbus himself had strictly forbidden, but was now doing himself. Anyway, after the admiral lay down to sleep apparently all the sailors did the same, for they must have been in wine, and the boy was the only one awake to steer the ship. Or did he go to sleep too? Anyway, this proved a fateful juncture for the *Santa Maria*. Around midnight the boy heard the rudder grate below. Apparently a wave had tossed the ship onto a sandbank. The boy cried out and Columbus and the crew awoke. Amidst the cursing and cries of despair from the sailors Columbus was frantically giving orders hoping that they would be able to get the ship off the sandbank. But the crew were thinking more of escaping to the *Pinta* and the *Niña* than of rescuing the *Santa Maria* and, with the waves pounding it, the caravel ran even more aground. In the end Columbus ordered the mast to be cut, to have all the stores and provisions removed to safety, and to have the ship lightened as much as possible.

At daybreak Columbus sent two of his sailors, Diego de Harana and Pedro Gutiérrez to ask the 'king' he had met, Guacanagari, for help. Columbus reports that when this king heard of the misfortune, he wept and sent the whole village to help. The *Santa Maria* could no longer be saved but the scores of canoes which turned up brought everything to land

6 He saw it on the Feast of St Thomas.

Fig.13   A reconstruction of Columbus' flagship, the *Santa Maria*

safely. Guacanagari sent to Columbus to say that he should
not be distressed at the loss of the *Santa Maria*, and that he,
Guacanagari, would give him everything he wanted. Columbus
in turn thanked Guacanagari for the help he received and
wrote that in the whole operation he had not lost as much
as a shoe-string. During the day Guanacagari had come
personally to help, and he had ordered his men to keep watch
during the night so that not a single thing should be stolen.

Yet this was just one of many occasions when Guacanagari
observed the greed of the strangers for gold. Even while the
villagers in canoes were trying to get the stores safely from
the wreck that cacique had seen Columbus bartering with some
of the boatmen for gold. This must have hurt his heart.
Columbus could certainly not have seen things that way.
Referring to Guacanagari in a letter to the king and queen of
Spain, and telling of this cacique's reaction to the loss of the

Santa Maria, Columbus wrote: 'He and all the people with him wept. They are a people so full of love and without greed and suitable for every purpose that I assure Your Highnesses there is no better race nor better land in the world.'

Columbus further told the sovereigns of Spain that although the people went naked, they were very refined in their dealings with each other, and so very orderly that it was a pleasure to see.

When Guacanagari had seen Columbus bartering hawks' bells for gold on the occasion of the wreck, he had told Columbus to keep one hawk's bell for him and he would pay for it in gold. He gave Columbus gold leaves as large as the hand, and when Guacanagari saw how joyful the admiral was, and realised that gold pleased Columbus more than anything else, he not only promised to get a great deal of gold for him but promised to show him the way to the mines in a province he called Cibao. Columbus was so delighted that he invited

Fig.14 The site of Navidad

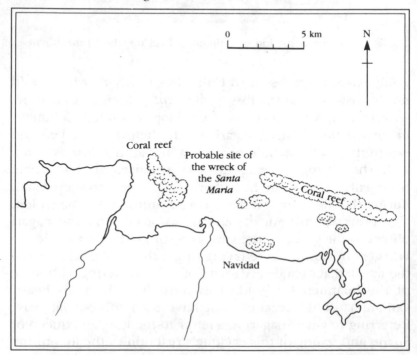

Guacanagari to dine with him that night on board his new
flagship, the *Niña*. After the dinner they both came ashore
and Columbus was done much honour.

Columbus gave Guacanagari a shirt to wear and a pair of
gloves. The shirt covered Guacanagari's nakedness, but this
was apparently of no importance to Guacanagari, for it was
the pair of gloves that he cherished, and the admiral reports
that the king was prouder of this than anything else in his life.
Guacanagari, dressed up, must have been the first native in
Haiti to wear clothes.

Columbus and Guacanagari ate together again the next
evening and Columbus was extremely impressed with the
manners, the tidiness, and cleanliness of Guacanagari, whom
he declared to be of good birth. He had particularly noticed
that when the king had finished eating, herbs were brought
to him and he rubbed his hands carefully with them. Among
the things they dined upon Columbus mentioned *casabi*,
which we know as cassava bread. After dinner Guacanagari
invited Columbus for a walk on the beach, and there he told
him horror stories of the man-eating Caribs, who constantly
harrassed his people. Columbus told him that the Caribs would
all be captured and bound, that dealing with them would be
no problem. To show his power, Columbus sent for a canon,
and when he had it fired, the natives were so terrified and
overwhelmed that they all threw themselves on the ground.
Guacanagari became even more convinced that these almighty
allies were people to cherish, and that the people of the earth
could have no power against these who came from heaven.

After the display of canon power Columbus was richly
rewarded, perhaps even more richly than he had expected.
The people gave him a large mask, which had great nuggets
of gold for the ears and eyes, and this gift was among other
gold ornaments, which the king placed on Columbus' head
and round his neck. Columbus, in his letter to the sovereigns
of Spain said that it was divine intervention which made his
ship run aground here, so that such good fortune should come
to him, and so that a settlement could be formed. He wrote:
'. . . In addition to this, so many things came to hand that
had I not run aground here, I should have kept out to sea

without anchoring at this place, because it is situated within a large bay and in that bay there are two more sandbanks; and on this voyage I would never have left people behind, and even if I had desired to leave them I could not have given the amount of supplies, stores, and provisions that would have been necessary, nor the material needed for making a fort.'

Columbus said this last because with the loss of the *Santa Maria* there was no question of the entire crew going back to Spain. The king, Guacanagari, offered to give him every help to accommodate some of the men. What made it easier for Columbus was that not everyone was in a hurry to make the journey back. One would have imagined that the Spaniards would have been longing to get back to Spain to see family and friends once more. True, many of them had spent a lot of time in jail, nevertheless they would certainly have missed the environment of a life so very different. For it was more than four long months they were away, and no one would have thought they would not have been eager to leave this wild, unfamiliar, unknown territory, even if it was for a while. Yet Columbus showed an interesting side of the picture when he wrote: 'It is very true that very many of the people who are with me have asked and petitioned that I give them permission to remain.'

The admiral goes on: 'Now I have ordered a tower and a fortress to be built, all very well done, and a large moat. Not that I believe it to be necessary for these people, for I take it for granted that with the men I have with me I could subdue all this island, which I believe to be larger than Portugal, and having more than twice the population.' Regarding the size of the two countries Columbus was wrong again. Portugal is nearly three-and-a-half times the size of the island of Haiti.

In respect to the people of Haiti, Columbus, allowing that they might have great numbers, added: 'But they are all naked and without arms and very cowardly beyond hope of change. It is right, however, that this tower should be built, and it must be as it must be, being so distant from Your Highnesses, and in order that they might realise the skill of the people of Your Highnesses, and what they can do, so that they may serve them with love and fear. So they have boards with which to

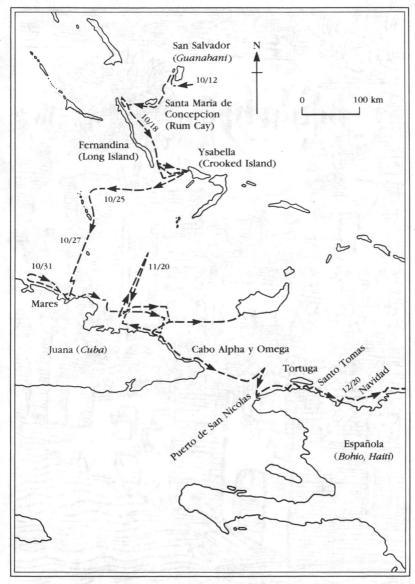

Fig. 15 Columbus' course through what we now call the Bahamas
to Juana (Cuba) and Española (Haiti)

construct the whole fortress, and provisions of bread and wine
for more than a year, and seeds to sow, and the ship's boat,
and a caulker, and a carpenter, and a gunner, and a cooper,

Fig.16   Building a fort at Navidad, from the Columbus letter, 1493

and many men among them who are zealous in the service of Your Highnesses, and who will give me the pleasure of finding the mine where the gold is collected.'

He named the site 'Navidad' as the shipwreck had happened on Christmas night, *Navidad* being 'Christmas' in Spanish.

The Cacique Guacanagari was very heart-broken over the prospect of Columbus' departure, and he made many attempts to detain Columbus, even promising to dress him in a suit of gold. Of course this was an easy way to detain Columbus, but the admiral must have known that this was a trick. He was eager to move. In fact he had spent a whole month in this small area in which he had first landed and where he had run aground. It was while here that Martin Alonzo Pinzón had deserted him, finding he was delaying too much to go in search of the king who had much gold. Martin Alonzo Pinzón who was commanding the *Pinta* had slipped away, and this had greatly worried Columbus, but at this time when the admiral was about to depart for Spain the *Pinta* came back.

Columbus was relieved but he did not forgive Martin Alonzo Pinzón, who he felt had tried to forestall him by going to

Fig.17   A reconstruction of the caravel *Pinta*

Baneque – where he got no gold, the admiral may have been glad to note. Martin tried to apologise to the admiral who did not want to hear him, accusing him of treachery and of being rude. In a letter reporting the matter to the king and queen of Spain Columbus said, 'I will not endure the acts of evil persons and men of little virtue who with small consideration presume to do what they will in opposition to him who did them honour.' However, through one of the *Pinta's* crew Columbus heard that Martin Alonzo Pinzón was able to barter the gold among his men. What excited Columbus was to know that there was a great amount of gold near to where they had been ship-wrecked. In his letter to the king and queen of Spain that night Columbus wrote: 'Thus . . . Sovereign Princes, I realise that Our Lord miraculously ordained that the ship should remain here, because it is the best place in all the island for forming a settlement, and nearest to the mines of gold.'

On that occasion he also told the sovereigns that a little to the south of Cuba, there was another great island, called 'Yamaye' by the natives, where there was so much gold that the people collected it from the mines in large nuggets. He said the natives had told him that Yamaye was ten days journey from Española, by canoe. One could see from Columbus' letters that although he was on the point of leaving he was no less obsessed with the thoughts of gold, and the natives, being cunning, knew that these were the stories he wanted to hear and kept on inventing them. Whether the stories of Yamaye, which the Spaniards rendered as Xamaica, and later as Jamaica – whether the stories of this island were completely false, or had some truth in them, we shall see later. Anyway, the time had come for Columbus to leave.

Before setting sail Columbus went to take his leave of Guacanagari and the cacique wept. Columbus commended to him the leaders of the men he was leaving behind – these leaders being Diego de Harana, Pedro Gutiérrez, and Rodrigo Escovedo. He was anxious to depart, for the sooner he left meant it would be the sooner he would return. He had no idea how much more of Haiti lay to the east and he had planned finding out – but not now. He was anxious to go and return quickly for his mind was on the thirty-nine men he was leaving at Navidad and, of course, his mind was on the bright nuggets of gold.

Columbus left Navidad on 4th January 1493. In his log he does not describe the parting, and not surprisingly, for it may have been emotional beyond words. Not speaking of the grief of Guacanagari and his other native friends, it must have been heart-rending to Columbus to leave thirty-nine of his men behind, in an island that he did not even know, and in an India that might shine with the promise of gold but could be savage and threatening. Maybe Columbus' deepest fears stemmed from the knowledge of the greed and ruthlessness of most of the Spaniards he was leaving behind. He had counselled them to take care and had asked Guacanagari to look after them. He left, with the ships' horns sounding goodbye, steering his new flagship, the *Niña*, carefully among the reefs, whilst keeping close to the coast.

He stopped at many other places along the way, naming as he went, rivers, capes, villages, harbours, bays – anything that caught his attention. Although he feared sailing so close to the shore – for if he lost another ship he did not know what

Fig.18 A reconstruction of the caravel *Niña*

he would do – he could hardly resist examining the easterly coast of Haiti, and of course to get more gold if there was any to be got.

Columbus spent more than a week sailing along the coast, and he was impressed with what a vast island it was. He followed the coast until he came to what he called a very high and beautiful cape of jagged rock, to which he gave the name 'Cabo del Enamorado', or 'Cape of the Beloved'. On the other side of this cape there was a deeply indented bay, which he called 'Puerto Sacro'. Today the cape is called Cape Samana, and the bay, Samana Bay. He landed at an islet in this bay but the people all fled. He also wanted to see if all that land was Española, or if what he was taking for a gulf, really separated the land he was seeing. He said that he was amazed that Española was so large.

He was anxious to leave this bay because as huge and as lovely as he thought it was, the bay was somewhat exposed to the north-east winds, and also he was intent on observing the conjunction of the moon with the sun, which, according to his calculations, was going to take place on 17th January. It was now 13th of January, nine days since he had left Navidad. He said he was also hoping to watch, on this occasion, the moon in opposition to Jupiter and in conjunction with Mercury, and the sun in opposition to Jupiter, which planet he said was the cause of great winds.

Some time after he left Puerto Sacro, seeing some people on a distant beach he anchored and sent a boat to shore to see if they could obtain some yams, of which the Spaniards were apparently fond. His boatmen met villagers with some bows and arrows, for which they exchanged gifts, and they asked one of these villagers if he would like to go to the big canoe and talk with the 'Admiral of the Ocean Sea'.

The man who went made Columbus recoil, for Columbus describes him as the ugliest of the natives he had seen. He was war-like in appearance and he wore his hair very long and drawn back and tied behind, and gathered in meshes of parrot feathers. Because of this the admiral judged the man to be one of the feared Caribs, who ate people. Nevertheless Columbus could not help asking about gold, which this villager called

Fig.19   Columbus' sketch map of north-west Española (Haiti)

tuob. Columbus declared that the villager understood gold only by that name, *tuob*, and not by *caono* as the people called it in other parts of Española. He said it was called *nozay* in the other islands. Without saying whether he had obtained the yams he had sent for – in fact they seemed completely forgotten – Columbus questioned the man at length as to where gold might be obtained but the man might not really have understood him. By this time, though, some of the native guides had apparently picked up a lot of Spanish, and the man, through these guides, told Columbus about Caribs further to the east, and spoke of another island even further to the east of the people of Caniba, a land which he told Columbus was called Matinino[7]. He said it was peopled only by women. The naïve Columbus believed this story.

The further east that Columbus had sailed the more he had met people who were in great fear of the Caribs and now he was properly convinced that there was a tribe who ate people. The stories told him were that boatloads of Caribs went from island to island eating as many people as they could catch. Although the admiral, in his eagerness to understand and converse with the 'Indians', had picked up many useful words, he found that the languages spoken in different parts were so different that even the guides he had with him aboard, some of whom came from the very country, did not follow everything that was said. Anyway, the villager with the long hair

7   Martinique

told him that *tuob* (gold) was obtainable, and Columbus gave him food and sent him back to shore with the request to bring back gold. When the boat, with accompanying Spaniards, reached the shore, about fifty warriors with bows and arrows emerged from the bushes. The villager made the other warriors lay aside their weapons and the Spaniards bartered their glass beads and coloured cloths for bows and arrows. But in the midst of the bartering the warriors attacked and tried to capture them, some running to the place where they had lain down their weapons. In the skirmish the Spaniards slashed one of their adversaries with a sword and wounded another with an arrow, causing the warriors to take flight.

The Spaniards returned to their caravel and when they told Columbus what had happened, he was sad that they had made enmity, but in a way he was happy that these people had had a taste of Spanish might. He said if those he left at Navidad were to find their way here they would be respected.

Feeling sure that the natives here were Caribs he was determined to capture some of them to take them to Spain, but when he sent men to the beach the next day, they were met by a great crowd offering peace and friendship. The cacique came too, and he visited the caravel with three of his aides, and Columbus made many gifts. Naturally Columbus asked about gold and the cacique promised to send him a golden mask.

After this happy interlude, Columbus began worrying about the state of his two remaining ships. The ships had been caulked very badly and were leaking. The admiral blamed the caulkers at Palos for their bad workmanship, but said, 'God who brought us to these Indias will lead us safely back home to Spain'.

The next day the cacique sent the mask of gold, and at the same opportunity a great deal of cotton and yams and bread were brought to the Spaniards. Columbus was impressed that the messengers all arrived with their bows and arrows, unlike what he thought of as the timid, cowardly people of other parts. Four young men came to the caravel and proceeded to give such a good description of the islands that Columbus wanted to take the men back to Spain with him. In a letter to the sovereigns of Spain he said, 'There is also a great deal of pepper in these parts and the people eat nothing without pepper. There is also excellent cotton. Fifty caravels could be loaded with it every year and sent to Spain.'

Despite his satisfaction, Columbus was eager to leave this place because the matter of the dispute on the beach was still on his mind. Also this was the first place he had seen bows and arrows in Haiti, and the thought of them did not please him. On entering the bay he had called it 'Puerto Sacro', but now as he left he re-named it 'Golfo de las Flechas', or 'Gulf of the Arrows'.

The natives had told him that Matinino also had gold and that the island lay to the east, and so when Columbus set sail from Golfo de las Flechas on Wednesday 16th January 1493, he had the immediate intention of calling at Matinino before taking the route to Spain. When he had gone some 64 miles one of the young men from Golfo de las Flechas told him, quite rightly, to alter his course to the south-east if he hoped to reach Matinino. But the sailors began to grumble saying that they wanted to go home, so Columbus, whether the young 'Indians' had been hoping to stay off in Matinino or not, continued on the direct route to Spain.

CHAPTER TWO
The Second Voyage

When Columbus arrived back in Spain the impact of his
adventure was overwhelming and incredible. He did not have
to try to convince anyone that he had been to the 'Indias';
the evidence that he had brought back with him moved Europe
to awe. He had packed the *Pinta* and the *Niña* with all manner
of things from the 'Indias' – trees and plants, fruit, root crops,
animals, birds, and he had brought back gold, not as much
as he had wanted to, but enough to inflame the minds of those
for whom he had sailed, and to make a lasting impression on

Fig.20 Spain united under Ferdinand and Isabella

the Court of Spain. But what Columbus had brought back that made the greatest impact of all on Europe, and removed any doubt that he had been to a strange and exotic land, were people – the inhabitants of a strange new world.

Explorers were aghast, and some embarrassed. Almost all were jealous. Scholars, as well as the people in the street, could hardly believe their ears, and those who saw for themselves could hardly believe their eyes.

To everyone, especially to explorers and geographers, this was the event of a life-time. The humble Genoese had scattered all those people who had been saying that the Earth was flat. He had reached the 'Indias' by sailing west, proving that the Earth was round.

As a whole, the reception of Columbus was very like euphoria. When he arrived at the Spanish court, which at that time was at Barcelona, Ferdinand and Isabella rose from their thrones to welcome him. They must have felt especially proud and fulfilled that they had shown a faith in Columbus that none of the monarchs of maritime Europe had shown. Isabella must have felt especially triumphant, for she had fought for Columbus from the start, against heated opposition from court advisers, and even from King Ferdinand himself.

There was no doubt at all that following Columbus' arrival in Spain in March 1493 there was no greater hero, and as the news travelled he was the most storied figure not only of Spain but of the entire 'Old World'. The king and queen of Spain lavished praise on Columbus not only as a great discoverer but as a leader of men. They heard with sadness of the loss of the *Santa Maria*, but they had high hopes that the establishment of the settlement at Navidad was the start of Spain's dominion across the ocean sea.

Yet the adulation did not change Columbus. He presented Ferdinand and Isabella with an account of his voyage with a prologue beginning: 'Most Christian and Most Exalted and most excellent and most mighty princes, King and Queen of the Spains, and of the islands of the Sea, our Sovereigns . . .' To which the sovereigns could with justice have replied: 'Most exalted, and most excellent, and most mighty Columbus,

Fig.21   Columbus bringing news of his explorations to
Ferdinand and Isabella of Spain

Admiral of the Ocean, and Discoverer of our Islands of the
Sea . . .'

Columbus, kneeling before the king and queen of Spain, and
surrounded by their ministers and advisers, must have been
reminded of those painful occasions when in that very setting
of the court he was ridiculed by all save the sovereigns, and
received active support only from Queen Isabella. Now he was
covered in glory, and not simply that, but he had covered all
Spain with glory. Because of the mission just completed Spain
would become the richest and most powerful nation under
the sun.

However, Columbus did not merely bask in his glory; he
began preparing straightaway for a second voyage. For
naturally he was as excited as anyone – in fact more excited
than most – about this new part of the world he had encountered, and he was most anxious to get back there, not only
to renew the explorations and hunt for gold, but to get
together with the thirty-nine men he had left at Navidad, see
what they had accomplished during his absence, but more than

ever to find that they had been safe and sound.

Columbus must also have thought of the cacique Guacanagari, who of all the people he had met in the 'Indias' was the one who had got really close to him. Although he had not yet found the Grand Khan he must have thought that, notwithstanding anything else, it was a wonderful thing discovering this cacique and all those gentle people. And no doubt Cacique Guacanagari

Fig.22   The islands Columbus 'discovered' and claimed for
Spain, from the Columbus letter, 1493

must have thought what a mystical thing it was to discover those men who had sailed from heaven in those great and magnificent canoes!

To Christopher Columbus Guacanagari would have replaced the Grand Khan, for a strange thing was that very little thought or mention was given now to this legendary figure, the splendour of whose domain was the chief cause of Columbus seeking the Indias. True, nowhere in the 'New World' had Columbus been able to see any such splendour as the Grand Khan was reputed to have. Guacanagari's headquarters may have been rich, but where were the jewels and ornaments of the court of Kublai Khan? The silks and satins and velvets, the shining ornaments and precious stones? It is not clear what was really Columbus' opinion of the relationship between the Grand Khan and the areas of his own exploration. What is certain is that neither he nor the princes of Spain, nor their advisers, nor the Spanish scholars of the time, nor indeed Europe as a whole, had any respect for the power of the Grand Khan. For were they not content that Columbus should 'discover' and claim his dominions for Spain?

Not only were the rulers and the ordinary people so disposed but even the Pope of Rome made his contribution. While Columbus was preparing for his second voyage the sovereigns of Spain applied to the Pope, Alexander VI, for a decree, called a 'Bull', confirming the new lands in the possession of Spain. The reason was that the other great Catholic nation, Portugal, was also seeking to discover the Indias, and the Spanish sovereigns foresaw the possibility of future disputes. The Pope, urging Ferdinand and Isabella to send further expeditions to complete their discoveries and to convert the 'Indians' to Christianity, granted the Bull, which was issued on 4th May 1493. The Bull stated: 'We . . . do give, concede, and assign forever to you and your successors all the lands and mainlands discovered, and which may hereafter be discovered, towards the west and south, whether they be situated towards India or towards any other part whatsoever, and give you absolute power in them, drawing, however, and fixing a line from the Arctic Pole, that is to say, from the north; to the Antarctic Pole, that is to say, to the south; which line must be distant from any one of the islands whatsoever, vulgarly called the Azores, or Cape Verde Islands, a hundred leagues towards the west and south – upon condition that no other Christian king or prince has actual possession of any of the islands found.'

New lands discovered to the east of this line were to belong to Portugal. Later, by the Treaty of Torsedillas, the sovereigns of Spain and Portugal agreed to shift this imaginary line 270 leagues to the westward.

On 15th March 1493 Christopher Columbus had arrived in Spain from what was thought to be the eastern outskirts of the Indias – and after spending about six months in Spain he was now ready to embark on his second voyage. There was, of course, no difficulty in getting a crew this time; there was no comparison with the first expedition when the jails had to be opened in order to get men to go with him. Because of the success of the first voyage, and the promise of great riches, all manner of people of all stations in life were rushing to make the trip, even buying their way, when they found this possible.

Unlike the first voyage when he had sailed from Palos, Columbus was going to set sail from the port of Cadiz, 100 kilometres to the south-east. That was not the only difference. When he had sailed from Palos the year before he had three ships and a crew of ninety men. Now his fleet consisted of seventeen ships and on board were 1,500 men. Among the vessels were three huge galleons, the rest being caravels, and among the men sailing with Columbus and who were to become famous, or infamous, were Ponce de Leon and Alonso de Hojeda.

Also, Columbus was leaving Spain with the earnest intention of starting a colony in the 'Indias' and on board were all sorts of seeds and plants and livestock, domestic pets such as dogs and cats, there were tools and other implements, and among the people sailing were craftsmen of all description. It appears that high among the list of priorities was the conversion of the 'Indians' to Christianity, and so there was a priest on board. Also on the ships were certain animals for the settlements, apart from the domestic pets, and although the Spaniards did not seem to have planned this, among these animals was a species destined to strike terror into the hearts of the natives of the newly-encountered lands. This creature was the horse. Columbus took twenty of them aboard, and wherever they went in these 'Indias', once they had their riders mounted, people fled in confusion, believing man and beast were one.

When Columbus left Spain on his second voyage he sailed out of the Mediterranean port of Cadiz with his colours flying in the wind, and with great cheering crowds behind him – and of course not only cheers but tears, for a great number of parents and sweethearts were left behind. The 'Admiral of the Ocean Sea' headed straight for the Canary Islands, as he had done on his first voyage. Here a great deal more provisions were taken on board, and also boarding were the first fowls, pigeons, sheep, goats and cattle to come to this newly-encountered part of the world. Columbus delayed somewhat in the Canary Islands, leaving the island of Ferro for the open sea on the 13th day of October in that year 1493. They sailed uneventfully throughout the voyage, encountering neither calm nor storm. Because a number of the 'Indians' had kept pointing to the south whenever Columbus has asked about gold, Columbus now set a course more southerly than he had done on his first voyage – although in fact the primary aim was to reach Navidad in the island of Haiti, or as he had called it, 'Española'. Spirits on board were high, and Columbus had offered a reward to anyone who spotted land first. After twenty days sailing, at about five o'clock on the dawn of Sunday 3rd November a pilot on the admiral's own flagship, *Santa Maria la Galante*, screamed out, 'Tierra!' and demanded his reward.

There were great cries of joy, as the message went from ship to ship. The excitement was all the more great as comparatively few of those aboard had had any experience of a long sea voyage before, and must have been terrified after so many days on the open sea. The fleet moved in the direction of the land which appeared like a mountain rising sheerly out of the water. The land looked lush and green. This was clearly a small

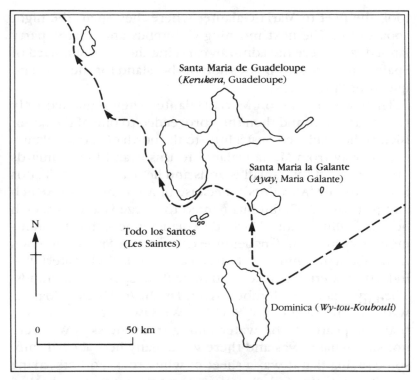

Fig.23   Santa Maria de Guadeloupe, Santa Maria la Galante
and Dominica

island and at just about the same time they saw a smaller island
not far to the north and a little to the east. This island was
flat, but also lush and green. To the mountainous island, which
was the first land the Spaniards had seen, Columbus gave
the name 'Dominica', meaning 'Sunday', because the day
happened to be Sunday. He called the other island 'Maria
Galante' his nickname for his flagship, which he loved.

   As the sun rose other islands began to appear on both sides
of the fleet, and he counted six islands in all. However it was
Dominica that he made for. He could see no harbour on the
eastern coast of the island, and in fact there was hardly even
a beach, the mountain rose up so sheerly from the sea. It was
also reported that Columbus was forced to turn away because
of the fierce natives of the island who threatened his ships.
Anyway, finding it difficult to land in Dominica the admiral

took the fleet to Maria Galante, where they spent the night aboardship. The next morning Columbus and a large party landed, and there the admiral, carrying the royal standard of Spain, formally took possession of the island for the king and queen of Spain.

They saw no one on Maria Galante. They remained only two hours there and then they proceeded to one of the larger islands they had seen, just a little to the north of Maria Galante. On his way from Maria Galante to this island the Spaniards saw a group of four small islands and he named them 'Todos los Santos', or 'All Saints'[1], because of All Saints' Day, which had just passed. Columbus named the large island to which he was sailing 'Santa Maria de Guadeloupe' after a famous monastery in Spain. Guadeloupe charmed the Spaniards when from about ten miles out they saw a beautiful waterfall – indeed a waterfall that seemed to be flowing from the clouds. The physician of Columbus' fleet, Dr Diego Alvarez Chanca, wrote to the Chapter of Seville: 'We saw it from so far off that it appeared to be water falling from the sky. We were not sure what it was and there were many bets aboard ship, some saying that it was a sheet of white rocks, others saying that it was a waterfall. When we came nearer to it, it showed itself completely, and it was the most beautiful thing in the world to see from how great a height and from what a small space so great a body of water was discharged.'[2]

Again there was the problem of finding a harbour. Approaching the island which he called Santa Maria de Guadeloupe at a point on the shore of the present village of Ste Marie, the admiral set about looking for a place to anchor. In the late evening of that day, 4th November, Columbus put down anchor in the cove now called Gran Anse.

There the Spaniards saw some dwelling places and went towards them, but the inhabitants, on seeing the strangers, fled into the bushes. Whether or not the news had previously come to them that a strange white tribe had appeared among the islands of the north, it is not known, but they must have

1 The islands, which became French, are known today as 'Les Saintes'.
2 These are the falls from the Great Carbet River, Guadeloupe.

Fig.24   Indians fleeing from Columbus, from the Columbus letter, 1493

been bewildered to see the strange, huge canoes approach their shores. As was said, when the Spaniards landed the inhabitants fled into the bushes. Columbus himself went into the houses, and he reported that in one of the them he saw two large parrots and a great quantity of cotton – some spun into cloth and some raw and ready to be spun. He was amazed at the spun cotton, especially the rugs. According to Dr Chanca, 'they were so well woven that they owed nothing to those of our country'. Columbus also saw magnificently-made earthenware and he saw articles of food. What appeared among the articles of food stunned him. For there was now stark evidence that he was in the land of the man-eaters. Here also lived the dreaded Caribs whom he had heard so much about! He brought away several bones of human arms and legs.

They went back to the ships and went along the coast, seeking a better harbour. Finding none, they spent the night aboard. In the morning, several of the captains landed with their detachments and went inland. There they encountered people for the first time and a great number of the people they encountered were already captives. Several of these were women, and they took many away. And now at last they began to learn a great deal about the natives of the island.

Columbus, by the use of signs and by speaking to his native guides – those 'Indians' he had taken to Spain with him – learned that the captives were held in raids that the Caribs had made on the Arawak islands, such islands as Cuba and Haiti. The women did not appear to be in danger of being eaten. The attackers usually carried off the women as wives, they said, but devoured the males.[3] The Spaniards did not see the Caribs and were told by the women that on that very day the men had left on a raiding expedition.

However, on one occasion the seamen saw several distant figures come to the beach and stare at the huge canoes with wonder, but when they tried to approach them these people fled.

Dr Chanca, in his letter to the Chapter of Seville, said: 'We were able to distinguish which of the women were natives and which were captives, because the Caribs wore on each leg two bands of woven cotton, one band fastened around the knee and the other around the ankle. By this means they make the calves of their legs large, and the above-mentioned parts very small, which, I imagine they regard as a matter of refinement.'

The Spaniards learned that the island they called Guadeloupe was 'Kerukera', that Dominica's name was 'Ceyre', and that the island Columbus had named after his ship, Maria Galante, was called 'Ayay'.[4]

Columbus and his men noted that the Carib weapon of

3   The Caribs in various parts differed slightly in habits. Some were apparently not cannibalistic, others ate parts of men in religious ceremonies, while it appears from what the women told Columbus that these Caribs ate the men not simply for religious reasons.
4   There are slight variations to these names as of course they had not been written down.

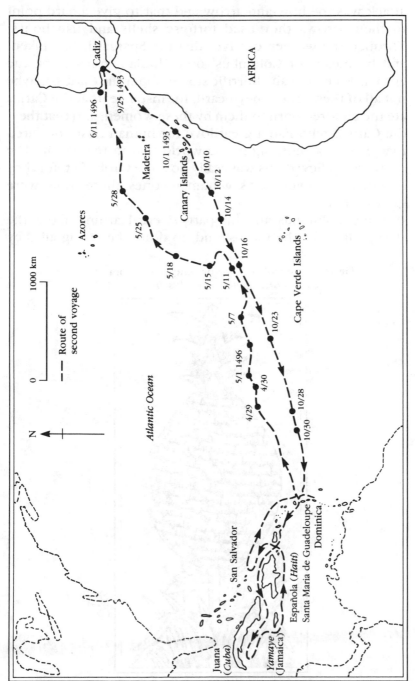

Fig. 25   The course of Columbus' second voyage

attack was the bow-and-arrow and that to give a hard point
to their arrows they used tortoise shells and fish bones.
Through the women captives that the Spaniards had taken,
and by means of Columbus' own 'Indian' translators, the
Spaniards heard many horrific stories about the Caribs, maybe
not all of them true. They heard, for instance, that the Caribs
ate the children born to them by these women, and that they,
the Caribs, who had a great love for human flesh, declared
that there was nothing in the world that tasted like it. The
Spaniards believed this was really how the Caribs felt, for they
said that wherever they saw human bones, these bones were
gnawed dry.

While Columbus and his party were learning about the
strange lives of the Caribs, and no doubt believing all they

Fig.26   The fruit *anana* or pineapple, from Oviedo's
La historia generale de las Indias, 1547

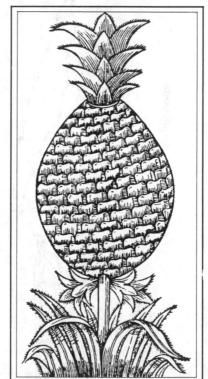

heard, a group of about 200 Spaniards who had ventured into the forests got themselves lost. The admiral sent out search parties with trumpets and horns blaring, but there was no success. In the end the group managed to emerge out of the forest at a seaside place, from where they were rescued. They had been lost for four days, forcing Columbus to remain in Guadeloupe six days in all. The group said that the forests were so thick that they could not see the stars from which to take direction and that had they not arrived at the coast it would have been impossible to get out of the forests.

The Spaniards, on the whole, loved this lush, green island. Having landed at the extreme southern point, in the mountainous section of the island, they had no idea that there was another part on the western side that was, in contrast, very flat. Here, incidentally, in Kerukera, was where, for the first time, the Spaniards saw and tasted the fruit, *anana*, which we call pineapple.

Having landed on the island on 4th November, it was not until six days later that they were able to lift anchor, taking with them the memory of a lovely island, yet an island of horrors because of its Carib people. In relation to the Caribs a new word was soon to be added to the Spanish language: the word *cannibal*.

Columbus set sail from Kerukera, the island he had named Guadeloupe, at daybreak on Sunday 10th November 1493, and he had the intention of heading straight for Haiti. He was anxious to get to Haiti again particularly because of the men he had left at Navidad. As a matter of fact he was quite annoyed about those who had got lost in the forests of Guadeloupe, and had even threatened to leave without them.

Michele de Cuneo, one of the men who sailed with Columbus on the second voyage, showed us another side of the 'pious' admiral when he noted that among the people Columbus took aboard from this Carib island were 'twelve very beautiful and plump girls, from 15 to 16 years old'.

From Kerukera, Columbus set a course which brought him directly along the island chain leading to Haiti, and although all credit is given to the 'discoverer' for finding these islands, there is evidence that it was the native guides who led him to them. Heading almost due north from Guadeloupe, but with a slight deviation to the westward, he came the next day upon what was a much smaller island which the girls aboard said was depopulated by the Caribs, so he did not call there. But as usual he was going to name the island, and being so much in love with his flagship, *Santa Maria la Galante*, this island, like the one he had just left, was going to be a 'Santa Maria' too. He named it 'Santa Maria de Montserrat' in honour of a famous monastery near Barcelona in Spain.

From this island he saw another one some distance easterly and a little to the north. He had no enthusiasm to go up to it, and maybe the girls aboard did not speak of it as a great attraction. He named it 'Santa Maria la Antigua' after the statue of a virgin in the cathedral at Seville. He had prayed before this statue just prior to leaving on this voyage.

Keeping on the north-westerly and curving course he came to a round piece of land, no more than a rock. This he named 'Santa Maria la Redonda'. It was still 11th November and that night his ships found shelter on the leeward side of a much larger island. Remembering that it was the eve of the feast of

Fig.27   From Santa Maria la Galante to San Cristóbal (Saba)

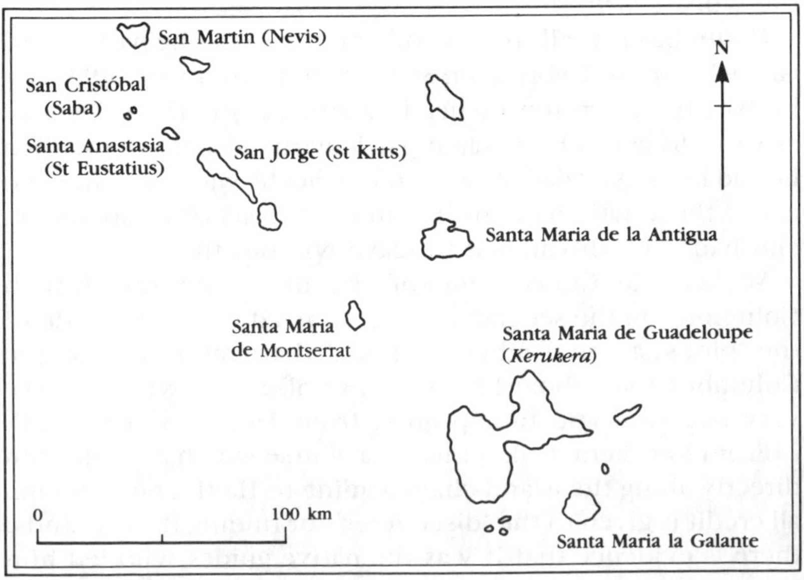

St Martin of Tours, he named this island 'San Martin'. However, the name San Martin was transferred to another island a few years later, and the original San Martin was given the name 'Nuestra Señora de las Nieves', the island we know as Nevis today.

From his anchorage off Nevis Columbus could see three lofty islands. One was just next to Nevis. Here there is uncertainty about the names Columbus gave. It seems that Columbus named the island next to Nevis 'San Jorge' and that it was only afterwards it was given the name 'St Christopher' the name of the patron saint of travellers, and also an allusion to the admiral himself, Christopher Columbus. He named the very next island to the northward after the virgin martyr, Santa Anastasia. This name suffered many variations and later, under the Dutch, it was rendered as 'Saint Eustatius'. It was the third of the three lofty islands that he called 'San Cristóbal', which is the Spanish version of 'St Christopher', the patron saint of travellers. But as was seen, later map-makers put this name against San Jorge, and San Cristóbal became 'Saba'.

Columbus, wanting to make up time, because of his having spent six days on Guadeloupe, did not land on any of the islands being mentioned. Also, he did not want to do any night sailing, for fear he missed any of the islands or ran aground. In addition, the nearer he drew to Haiti – and sailing by the stars and by his own reckoning he had a good idea as to where he was – the more anxious he became to see the men he left at Navidad. For one thing he was nervous to see if all of them were safe and well, and then he wanted to hear all the news, and of course he felt sure that by now they had discovered the mines of gold. As regards the rich king of Baneque, if he knew at all the men he had left behind it was sure now to be a case not of the king who had much gold but of the Spaniards who had much gold. He could hardly wait to be in Haiti again.

It was 12th November when Columbus went past the islands we know as Nevis, St Kitts, and St Eustatius, and he changed course to almost due west to find the island that his native guides must have directed him to, and which they told him was called Ayay. They sighted Ayay on the 14th, and of course, Columbus, seldom satisfied with the native name for any place, called it 'Santa Cruz' – in English, 'Holy Cross'. Much later, under the French, the name was translated to 'St Croix'.

This island, Ayay, appeared to the Spaniards to be unique. They reported it to be thoroughly cultivated and densely populated. However, as pleasant as Ayay, or Santa Cruz, seemed, when the Spaniards were sailing into it they were sailing in to their first fight in this part of the world; that is, if the little skirmishes of the first voyage are to be ignored.

Columbus sailed into the island from the eastern, pointed end. The fleet anchored at about midday, and Columbus sent an armed boat ashore before which the people fled. The Spaniards, as usual, took some captives. Then a canoe containing seven people – four men, two women, and a boy – sailed up, stupefied by the Spanish fleet. The Spaniards right away tried to capture them, and according to Dr Chanca, 'with great courage they took up their bows, the women as well as the men'. Dr Chanca adds, 'And I say with great courage because they were no more than four men and two women, and ours were more than 25, of whom they wounded two.' One of the wounded Spaniards died from the fight.

Michele de Cuneo, whose letters add greatly to the knowledge of what took place on the second voyage, declared that he personally captured 'a very beautiful Carib girl', who he said, Columbus allowed him to keep. This throws a little bit more light on Columbus' attitude to the relationship between the Spaniards and the women of these 'Indias', a matter on which the chronicles are so silent.

Anyway, Columbus, because of the fiery introduction to Ayay, or Santa Cruz, named this spot 'Cabo de la Flecha' or 'Cape of the Arrow'. He did not remain long here, he arrived on Thursday 14th November and he quickly lifted anchor and took a course not only due north but north-north-east, clearly being told by his guides that there were islands in that direction. Not long after his departure from his anchorage he saw the silhouette of the islands mentioned but it was not until the evening of Saturday 16th November that he arrived among them, a little archipelago. Although he must have been told about these islands – some no larger than rocks – he was nevertheless surprised at their number. Straightaway he was

Fig.28   Once Mil Virgenes (Virgin Islands) and Santa Cruz (St Croix)

reminded of Santa Ursula and her eleven thousand sea-going virgins and he named the islands 'Once Mil Virgenes' (Eleven Thousand Virgins). These islands soon became known as the Virgin Islands.

The admiral and his fleet remained among these myriad islands throughout Saturday and Sunday 16th and 17th November, and turning back the next day to sail due west he came upon a little green island that he named 'Graciosa' after the mother of a good friend, Allesandro Geraldini. The island was later called 'Vieques'.

As pleasant and lush as Graciosa looked Columbus must have been anxious to move on, not only because he was impatient to get to Haiti, but because his 'Indian' guides must have been telling him of the large island not far to the west, known as 'Borinquen'. Borinquen lay just between them and Haiti. It was in full view and Columbus set off at once. The closer they approached the more the island looked large, and lush, and lovely, and as expected, Columbus had already named it, disregarding its Arawak name, and, of course, he had already committed it to the royal sovereigns of Spain. His name for this island was 'San Juan Bautista' in honour of St John the Baptist, a saint much loved in his native Genoa. (A little later

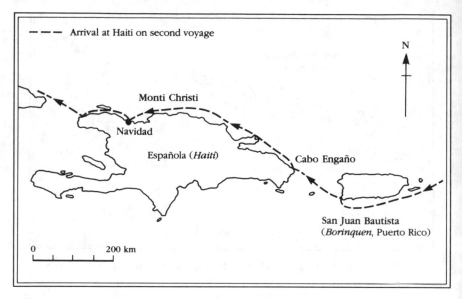

Fig.29   San Juan Bautista (Puerto Rico) to Española (Haiti)

one of Columbus' shipmates, Ponce de Leon, founded a city on the northern coast, facing a superb harbour, or port. Ponce called the city 'San Juan de Puerto Rico'. The city remained 'San Juan', but for the country as a whole the last two words sufficed: 'Puerto Rico'.)

But on the day in question, Tuesday 19th November 1493, Columbus' fleet sailed all along the spectacular southern coast of Borinquen. The admiral over-estimated the size of this island, deeming it to be as big as Sicily, when in fact it is just one fifth of the size of Sicily. However, Dr Chanca had an accurate measure of the extent of its south coast, which he declared was 30 leagues long (just over 100 miles).

Sailing all day they covered this distance between dawn and dusk anchoring for the night off a cape on the extreme western side of the island's south coast, to turn north next morning and make sail for a pleasant and sheltered harbour called 'Boqueron'. Arriving there on Wednesday, they spent that day and the next obtaining water and provisions. As was now the pattern, although the whole region must have now heard of the presence of the white-skinned men, the natives fled at their approach. Some of the Spaniards who ventured into the

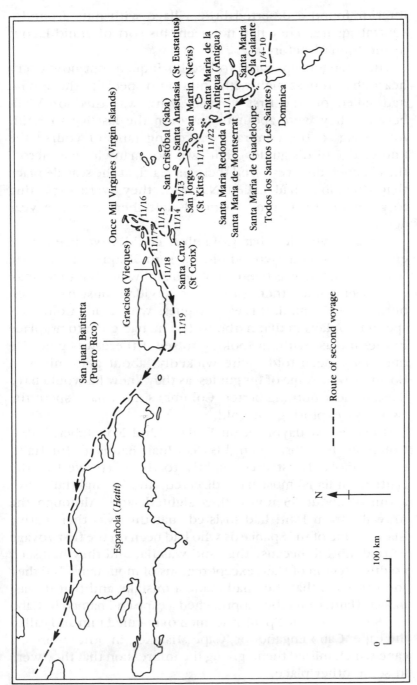

Fig.30   Santa Maria la Galante to Española (Haiti)

interior found a deserted little village with huts around a central square. They had not seen this sort of grand layout in the 'Indias' before.

The strangers appeared to like Borinquen, but now every heart aboard beat high with emotion. Especially those who had sailed on the first voyage. Why was this so? Well, because they were about to leave on the last leg to Haiti. According to the admiral's reckoning (and of course the knowledge of his guides) Haiti was not many leagues across the channel, due west. And there, in Haiti, at the seaside place that Columbus had called Navidad, they were expecting to greet the thirty-nine Spaniards left there almost a year ago.

It was a wonder that Columbus could have been calm enough to spend two whole days in Boqueron Bay. He declared that he was taking in wood and water but there may have been some other reason, for Navidad must have been burning in his mind. It is easy to guess what made Columbus spend two days in that harbour. For he had gone to no place in the 'Indias' without looking to see if there was gold. He must have been told, quite wickedly, about gold mines in Borinquen by some of his guides, as they knew he would have liked to hear nothing better. Columbus must have spent the two days exploring for gold.

However, at daybreak on Friday 22nd November, 1493, Columbus left Borinquen, his 'San Juan Bautista', for Haiti, his Española. He steered slightly to the north-west as the Haitian 'Indians' must have directed, and by nightfall, after a run of about 65 miles, they sighted land. Although the Arawaks from Haiti had insisted that this was their native island, some of the Spaniards who had been on the first voyage were doubtful, because this land was flat and they had seen no other region of Haiti except regions of mountains. But they soon realised that they had made a mistake and that it was, in fact, Haiti. Columbus approached a cape and named it 'Cabo San Rafael', but the Spanish seamen over-ruled him and called the cape 'Cabo Engaño' or 'Cape Mistake', in other words, a cape which misled them, giving the impression that they were in some other place.

Again in Española

The cape might have deceived them but what stunned them, and suddenly killed their joy at nearing Navidad, was what they discovered at a place they had named Monti Christi, just a few leagues before they reached Navidad. While looking for a site more convenient than Navidad the men found two corpses bound with ropes, and the next day two more were discovered. The bodies were in such a state of decomposition that they were unrecognisable, but one thing confirmed the deep suspicion of the Spaniards. On one of the faces were the remnants of a Spanish-style beard.

It was Wednesday 27th November and the Spanish fleet made all speed to Navidad. They reached Navidad at nightfall, and Columbus, mindful of how the *Santa Maria* had run aground in the dark, decided to remain the night at anchor outside the fort and proceed to it the next morning. But eager to get a response from the fort they lit flares and fired cannons. No flares were forthcoming from where the fort of Navidad would have been situated, and there was no answering salute. This plunged the Spaniards into deep dejection and grief.

Later that night a canoe bearing, among others, a cousin of Guacanagari, approached the Spanish fleet and told Columbus that Guacanagari had sent greetings but that he was wounded and could not come. The cacique's cousin offered Columbus two gold masks – one for him and the other for a 'captain who had been with him on the other voyage'. Naturally the Spaniards were quick to ask about the men they had left behind, and they were told the Spaniards were well, except that some had died of sickness, and that others had been killed in a quarrel. However, the interpreting guide, one returning from Spain and who had been christened Diego Colón, managed to get another story, but Columbus refused to believe that the timid, defenceless 'Indians' could have wiped out the men of his fort.

Columbus must have been naïve, for only thirty-nine men had been left behind, and with the Spaniards' cruelty and greed for gold, it would not have taken much for several thousands of people from the surrounding country to liquidate them.

Anyway, the next day, Thursday 28th November, the Spaniards arrived at Navidad to find the fortress burned to the ground and no sign of life whatsoever, at least no sign of Spanish life. According to Dr Chanca, the few 'Indians' that ventured around moved about very stealthily. Columbus and his Spaniards sent a message to Guanacagari to come aboardship and give an account of what had happened. Guanacagari did not turn up. Dr Chanca tells that while walking on the beach with Columbus the next day they came to a village from which the people fled on seeing them. Inside the houses of these villagers the Spaniards found many articles plundered from the fort. When the Spaniards returned to the site of the fort some bartering 'Indians' showed them the bodies of eleven Spaniards lying where they had been killed. They said that a neighbouring cacique, called Caonabó, had attacked and killed the Spaniards and that Guacanagari had been wounded in that battle. Dr Chanca added: 'but at once they began to complain that the Spaniards had taken three or four women apiece, whence we believed that the evil which had befallen them was out of jealousy'.

While thinking of the Navidad affair Columbus sent out two caravels, one to the eastward and one to the westward, officially in search of a permanent site for settlement, but also, most certainly, to do some spying. The one that went to the westward, commanded by Melchior Maldonado, sailed into a bay and while he was supposed to be looking at a site he received a message from Cacique Guacanagari to come to see him. He found Guacanagari stretched out in a hammock, apparently suffering from an injured thigh. Guacanagari expressed an eagerness to see Columbus and declared Caonabó had killed the Spaniards at Navidad.

Columbus' response was a show of force, with more than a hundred armed Spaniards in battle array escorting him to see Cacique Guacanagari. Marching to the music of pipes and the beating of drums, they must have been a frightening sight to the villagers, but it did not deter Guacanagari from sticking to his story that it was the hostile cacique whose forces had attacked and killed the men. The crafty Columbus, on the pretext of rendering expert treatment, had Dr Chanca unroll the bandage from the cacique's leg. Dr Chanca declared that there was no sign of any wound on the leg, although he said Guacanagari 'was foxy and pretended that it hurt him greatly'.

Whatever it was, Guacanagari certainly appeared to have suddenly had a great ease for he not only visited Columbus on board the *Maria Galante* that very evening, but dined sumptuously. On that occasion he was shocked out of his wits when he saw a horse. As was said before, sheep and horses as well as all kinds of other animals were aboard on that second voyage. That instance of the dinner was the very first time a horse was seen by anyone from these 'Indias', except Columbus' guides.

When Guacanagari returned to land Columbus held a meeting among his men to decide what should be done about the massacre. A priest among them, Fray Buil, along with a number of others, said Guacanagari was guilty and should be seized and put to death. Columbus did not feel Guacanagari was guilty, and in any case he did not want to be so rash as to put a cacique to death, thus inviting an uprising against him. He felt the best thing was to wait until both sides got to know each other's language better and then the truth would be known.

Shortly afterwards, through the keenness of Columbus' guides, some of the silent inhabitants of the area began talking of what had happened. No sooner had Columbus turned his back for Spain, they said, than the Spaniards left behind at Navidad began to quarrel over women and gold. As the story was told, Rodrigo de Escovado, the secretary, and Pedro Gutiérrez, the royal butler, killed Jacome, a Genoese seaman, and joined a gang seeking women and gold. Caonabó, the cacique of a province called Maguana, apprehended the gang and put the Spaniards to death and then attacked Navidad to wipe out the source of the trouble. In the meantime most of Navidad's garrison had broken up into gangs, the story went, and only ten men remained to guard the fort, under Diego de Harana. These ten could not withstand the fury of Caonabó's men, and Navidad was swept away. The other gangs and stragglers were soon killed off, closing that episode.

The Spaniards set sail from Navidad in search of a good area for settlement. They could have found suitable places near where they were but the admiral kept hearing of mines of gold and wanted to establish the settlement near to the reputed mines. After setting sail they found a tough easterly wind and could make little impression against it. But they proceeded onwards, and on 2nd January 1494, the fleet anchored in a promising location. There was a sheltered harbour and a small plain on which a city could be built. Yet the admiral wanted to move on, just in case there was something better, and of course he wanted to see as much of the country as he could. And, most important of all, he hoped he would accidentally come across a mine of gold. But he was forced to remain there, for the people were tired and wanted to go no further. The admiral had already spent a month beating about for a site. Then too the livestock were dying. Many pleaded with Columbus to settle there. However, Dr Chanca, a close associate of Columbus, did not attribute the founding of the settlement there to any such thing. He wrote: 'It pleased Our Lord that through the foulness of the weather, which would not let us go farther, we had to land on the best harbour and fine fishing, of which we stood in great need owing to the lack of meat'. Whatever it was, whether, as is likely, all these views prevailed, the point was that Columbus remained on the site and established a settlement – the first non-indigenous settlement in what the Spaniards were already calling the 'New World'. Columbus named the settlement 'Ysabella', in honour of the queen of Spain.

Columbus was elated when, having established Ysabella he was told by natives of the region that mines of gold lay nearby. He was very keen and anxious, for the large fleet of seventeen ships had to return to Spain soon, and to return them with a few barrels of gold would show the sovereigns that the voyage had already paid for itself several times over. He was most anxious to have some gold to send back, especially so as he had promised this, having anticipated that the men at Navidad would have already found the mines of abundant gold. Part of the fleet of seventeen was to have been sent back to Spain right away but Columbus held the ships back just in case he had something valuable to send with it. Then without delay and with the help of the guides he sent an expedition inland. This expedition was headed by Alonso de Hojeda.

Hojeda, of whom Las Casas says, 'He was always the first to draw blood wherever there was a war or a quarrel', had distinguished himself in this way sufficiently in many little enterprises on the voyage to cause Columbus to select him for the expedition. He left on his assignment on 6th January 1494, and he was in charge of about two dozen men and accompanied by native guides. They crossed the southern Cordillera into the great central valley of Haiti and claimed to have encountered streams which brought gold down from the high range. But the weather turned bad and a swollen river blocked their way. Hojeda turned back to the nearest village where he was told there was really abundant gold in the high range, and they presented him with large nuggets of gold to prove the point. However, not being able to press either forward, or uphill, he turned north towards the coast and regained Ysabella on 20th January.

Columbus was elated with the news that gold could be had. According to Cuneo, 'The Lord Admiral wrote to the king that he was hoping to be able shortly to give him as much gold as the iron mines of Biscay'. But of course the letter did not go for he still chose to hold back the fleet. Would it not be better to despatch barrels of gold to Spain rather than merely talk about gold?

Eventually, though, Columbus could hold back the fleet no more, because of an emergency which occurred among his men. About half of them fell severely ill and Dr Chanca diagnosed that the trouble was the food of the 'Indias' that the Spaniards were not yet accustomed to. So Columbus decided to send the fleet home right away so that Spanish food as well as medical supplies could come as quickly as possible.

On 21st February 1494 twelve of the seventeen vessels left for Spain. This fleet, which Columbus despatched under the orders of Antonio de Torres, arrived at the Spanish coast after only twenty-five days. It anchored at Cadiz a little later, on 7th March 1494.

Despite the fact that Columbus was not able to send back to Spain anything like the amount of gold he had hoped to

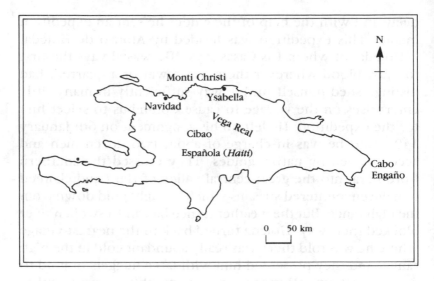

Fig.31   Española (Haiti) under Columbus 1492 – 1500

send, the fleet still returned with an impressive amount of the precious metal, as well as with cinnamon and pepper, samples of the timber of the 'Indias', dozens of parrots, and a good number of 'Indians', many of whom did not survive the voyage.

The five vessels that Columbus retained were his own flagship *Maria Galante*, the *Niña,* now a veteran; the *Gallega*, and two little caravels, the *San Juan* and the *Caldera*.

The story of what transpired after Columbus founded Ysabella is the story of how the Spaniards set about colonising and exploiting their 'New World'. This could be said to have started in earnest on 12th March 1494, when the admiral led an expedition in force across country, south from Ysabella. The expedition, which included all but a few left behind to garrison Ysabella, set out in military formation and with banners flying and trumpets blasting, and protected by crossbow-men, and by the gleaming swords of cavalry troops and foot soldiers. The Spanish warriors marched valiantly into the interior to what must have been the great surprise of the native peoples. It was the first time they had seen anything like it and none could have even imagined their own warriors launching an attack on the intruders. But in any case they were too stunned to do anything.

It was wonderful countryside the Spaniards were marching into, and when they were approaching the area of the Cibao, the location of the reputed gold mines, they entered a valley that Columbus described as being beautiful beyond words. He was profoundly moved by it and called it Vega Real (Royal Plain).[5] Samuel Eliot Morison who spent much time following the tracks of Columbus, wrote: 'My own first view of this Vega Real, at a season when the *madre de cacao*[6] trees put forth their pink blossoms, is one of the most memorable sights in my long wanderings over the routes of Columbus'.

It was a most successful expedition, and the natives in these parts, who had already met Hojeda, came in great numbers to see Christopher Columbus, whom they called *Guamiquina* or 'the great cacique of the Spaniards'. They brought gifts of all sorts, especially of gold, which gifts Hojeda had truthfully told them that the 'men from heaven' liked more than anything else.

Columbus built a fort on one of the hills of the Cibao and the Spaniards marched out again to Ysabella on 21st March 1494. They arrived at Ysabella on 29th March after several days of bad weather, and they were certainly not looking as impressive as when they had left. But the welcome of trumpets and musket shots must have excited their hearts.

Along with the establishment of Ysabella, this was the first impressive beginning of Spanish colonisation in the so-called 'New World'. Columbus spent a great deal of time in overland exploration as well as in administration of the settlement, Ysabella, and as will be seen, it was not until 1496 that this his second spell in the 'Indias' came to an end. Quite apart from the fact that this Genoese was not completely accepted by his men, which was bound to make his administration of Ysabella difficult, Columbus was by no means a great administrator, and his problems were many. The fact that he proved sensitive to criticism, that he was strong-willed, and also had

5   *Vega* is the flat land on the banks of a river.
6   Immortelle trees.

a persecution complex, made the job extremely difficult, and won him enemies on all sides.

So after he returned from the Cibao he decided that there was a lot more work to do and that his most important business was to get into his ship again and find new, and he hoped, rich lands, instead of just staying at Ysabella and having to treat with his jealous and vicious companions. That was how he saw it. So he left his brother Diego in charge, and set off with a chosen crew. He knew exactly in which direction he was going. He was heading for two large islands, one larger than Haiti, which he had seen before and explored a little; and another, smaller than Haiti, but which had almost as big a name so far as his expectations were concerned. He had heard of this island on his first voyage, and was anxious to go there now to collect the large nuggets of gold that he had heard of.

CHAPTER THREE
Further Explorations on the Second Voyage

Columbus left Ysabella on 24th April 1494, to continue his exploration of the 'Indias' and his mind was first of all on what he thought to be the mainland. He had seen this land in December 1492 when he was making for Haiti, and his native guides, who told him its coast was endless, seem to have given him the impression that this must be the mainland of the 'Indias'.

He took with him the little *Niña* as flagship, as well as the *San Juan* and the *Caldera*. He had twenty-five men with him on the *Niña*, chief of whom were the pilot Francisco Niño (of the family who owned the *Niña*), Alonso Medel, as master, and Juan de la Cosa, the chart-maker. The *San Juan* had a crew of fifteen aboard, with Alonso Roldán as master. The *Caldera* carried fourteen persons, with her master being Cristóbal Pérez.

The fleet headed westward and after four days sailing it reached the north-west tip of Haiti, and from there the coast of Cuba lay 45 miles in the distance, slightly to the north-west. The fleet took just one day to cross the passage, and they reached the cape which on his first voyage Columbus had named Alpha and Omega.

Once again, Columbus formally took possession of this land, which he had done more than once before on his first voyage. It will be recalled that he had named it Juana, after a daughter of Queen Isabella. Cuba, of course, much vaster than any of the islands he had so far seen, had many flourishing caciques, yet the only caciques that seemed to matter to Columbus were Ferdinand and Isabella of Spain. He did not even seem to bother anymore about a great and powerful Khan, although he believed he had at last reached the mainland of Asia. On the question as to whether this was the mainland or not one of his companions, Andrés Bernáldez, said in a letter to a friend: 'For you should know that this is the extreme headland of terra firma corresponding to Cape St Vincent in Portugal at the west. Between these two capes is contained all the world's population, so that if one should set forth by land from Cape St Vincent, one could always go eastward without crossing any part of the Ocean Sea until one arrived at Cape Alfa and Omega.' (As strange as it would seem, it took more than a decade for Europe to realise how wrong this statement was. No wonder that when the conquistadore, Vasco Nuñez de Balboa, saw the Pacific Ocean in 1513, he rushed upon it, sword in hand, to claim it for Spain.)

From Cape Alpha and Omega, today's Cape Maisi, Columbus made for Cuba's south coast. The day was 30th April. He stayed in the beautiful bay now called Guantanamo and he was off again at sunrise the next morning, that first day of May in 1494. As he sailed along the coast with the high mountains of what is now called the Sierra Maestra close beside

Fig.32   Juana (Cuba), Yamaye (Jamaica) and Española (Haiti)

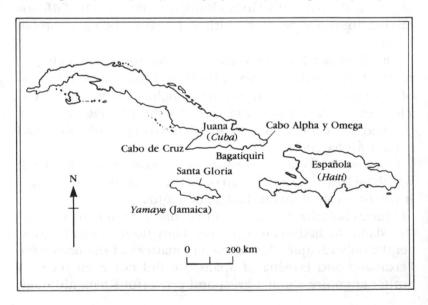

Fig.33   An Indian cacique of the island of Cuba addressing Columbus.
Drawn by B. West, engraved by F. Bartolozzi, 1794

him, great numbers of the native 'Indians' came to the water's edge to greet him, and some paddled out in canoes. Naturally they had all heard of this tribe wandering about their waters, and one report said they offered the Spaniards cassava bread and calabashes of water, while at the same time crying out, 'Eat and drink, men from heaven.'

The next place in which they cast anchor was where the sierra parted and a channel nearly 200 yards wide took them into the impressively beautiful bay on which today stands the city of Santiago de Cuba. What the Spaniards saw at the time was a little village called Bagatiquiri. Diego Colón, the 'Indian' who was baptized in Spain, was very happy to interpret what these people were saying to the eager Columbus, but he did not give Columbus the news he wanted to hear. The people had abundant fish and cassava bread but they had no gold. Columbus left Bagatiquiri and sailed on, and on Saturday 3rd May he reached the end of that scimitar-like coast, and he called the cape there 'Cabo de Cruz', the name it bears today.

Instead of turning northwards round Cabo de Cruz to pick up the rest of Cuba's southern shore, Columbus used Cabo de Cruz as a jumping off point for a journey south. For since he was on his first voyage he had heard of an important island to the south of Cuba, an island of large nuggets of gold. Indeed what made him seek the island now with even more enthusiasm was because while sailing down Cuba's scimitar shore he had heard even more about the riches of that island. One does not know if in answer to Columbus' questions, the villagers embellished, as usual, and told him just what he wanted to hear, but the island the name of which he sometimes wrote down as 'Yamaye', and sometimes as 'Xamaica', became as bright as a beacon in his mind.

However, as they set off a terrible storm broke out and after battling the storm for forty-eight hours, with the wind ripping off the sails and leaving the caravels under bare poles they reached Xamaica, arriving at about the middle of its north coast. The date was Monday 5th May 1494, when they approached the island, later called Jamaica. Nearing the coast the Spaniards were surprised at the virile beauty. The island radiated enchantment and it presented itself mountainous and stark and green. Columbus eased his fleet into a bay, now known as St Ann's Bay, but which he called 'Santa Gloria'.

Columbus happened to be extremely excited over this island and not simply because of the stories of nuggets of gold. In all the 'Indias' he had visited, possibly only Haiti drew more fulsome praise from him. Keeping in mind the fact that he was very much prone to exaggeration it is nonetheless interesting to see his comments. He wrote to Ferdinand and Isabella: 'It

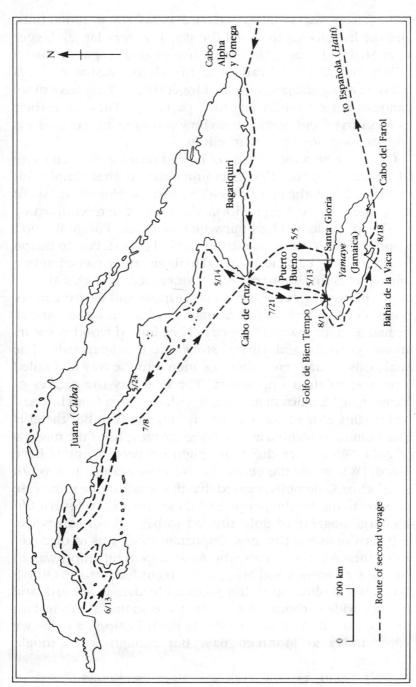

Fig.34 Columbus' explorations of Juana (Cuba) and Yamaye (Jamaica) on his second voyage

is the fairest island that eyes have ever beheld, mountainous, and the land seems to touch the sky. It is very large – bigger than Sicily[1]. It has a circumference of 800 leagues (I mean miles), and all full of valleys and fields and plains . . . It is full of very big villages, very near together . . . They have more canoes than elsewhere in these parts . . . They have their canoes carved and painted both bow and stern with ornaments so that their beauty is marvellous . . .'

Of course he wrote this after he had seen a great deal more of Jamaica. On this first encounter the admiral simply felt enchanted with the place in which he found himself. He spent only one night at Santa Gloria, departing the next morning to a deeply indented harbour which he called 'Puerto Bueno', a port still carrying the name the admiral gave it. Puerto Bueno might certainly have been a good harbour, as the name implies, but so far as the Spaniards were concerned, that was all. For at this place the people, carrying weapons and wearing head-dresses of feathers, gave Columbus as hostile a welcome as he had seen for many a long day. They hurled wooden spears at the caravels and threw stones at the Spaniards. The Spaniards in turn sent crossbow-men into the fray and killed a number of their opponents. The next day the natives of Yamaye or Xamaica made peace with the 'men from heaven' by bringing gifts of cassava bread, fruit and fish. But the gifts that Columbus wanted and never got were gifts of the nuggets of gold. 'Where are the large bright nuggets,' he must have asked, 'Where are the gems of this lovely island?' It was not long before Columbus realised that this was just one more case of 'sweet-talk' by the peoples of these islands. The stories of the large nuggets of gold proved to be without substance.

If for Columbus the most important thing was to discover gold, then for the annals, the most important thing was to encounter Xamaica and bring it into recorded history. On 9th May 1494, Columbus sailed 34 miles further westward, and found a wide harbour. The weather was so fine at this instant that he named the place 'Golfo de Buen Tempo', a place we know today as Montego Bay. But enough was enough.

1 Sicily is nearly two and a half times bigger than Jamaica.

Xamaica, having no gold, lost the radiance of its charms for Columbus, and the admiral set sail for Cuba again, touching Cabo de Cruz on 14th May.

Columbus explored the south coast of Cuba, calling at 'Indian' villages, putting in at harbours, threading through the myriad islands which lie easterly on Cuba's south coast, looking at rivers and other natural features and naming them as he went, and of course looking for gold also; and in the end the admiral sailed almost the whole of the 500-mile coastline, when, feeling confirmed in his belief that Cuba was no island but a peninsula of Asia, he turned back.

He began the return voyage on 13th June and after a most eventful passage with extremely bad weather, he reached Cabo de Cruz on 18th July. This was the point from which Columbus had broken journey to find the island of Xamaica (Jamaica), and having reached here again he, oddly enough, again set off for Jamaica, reaching the harbour he had called Golfo de Buen Tiempo on 21st July.

Columbus explored the coastline to advantage on his second visit to Jamaica, and after leaving Golfo de Buen Tiempo where he seems to have spent about ten days, he turned westward on 1st August, rounded the western end of the island, and took the south coast. On this journey he called at several villages, no doubt still clinging to the idea of bright nuggets, and on 18th August he entered a large and deeply-indented harbour which he named 'Bahia de la Vaca' (now Portland Bight).

At this port a most spectacular incident took place. According to one of the Spaniards, Andrés Bernáldez, the people greeted Columbus in a friendly way, and a cacique from a large village came with food supplies and had a long conversation with him through the interpreter, Diego Colón. Columbus must have spoken of the glories of Spain and of Ferdinand and Isabella, and Diego Colón must have embellished this to a magnificent degree for the cacique was stunned with wonder. Next day, after Columbus' fleet had left Bahia de la Vaca, the Spaniards saw three canoes coming to overtake them. The occupants of the canoes, magnificently dressed with colourful feathers and standards, some with painted faces, and many of them adorned with golden ornaments, were none other than the cacique who had spoken to Columbus, his wife and children, and his retinue. They got on board Columbus' vessel even before the admiral realised it, and when the native chief saw Columbus he went to him in great joy. The cacique said that the story of Castile which Columbus told him through Diego Colón was such a wonderful and intriguing story that he and his family proposed to go home with him to see the great and wonderful land from which the Spaniards came, and to talk to those great caciques, Ferdinand and Isabella. Columbus was very touched but could not accede to the request. Firstly, he was going back to his settlement in Haiti, he said, and he had no idea when he would be sailing to Spain. Then, he must have asked himself, would his uncouth seamen know how to restrain themselves with these royal ladies and act as men from heaven? Also, another point to consider: he had painted such a beautiful picture of Spain that it must have appeared a paradise, and in any case he was sure that in the cacique's mind heaven and Spain was the same place. But Spain was on earth and on earth there was no paradise. Disillusionment was bound to set in. And would not these naked 'Children of Eden' and of eternal summer, wither and die of cold in that alien land? Columbus politely declined the honour and sent the cacique and his family back to their canoes.

From Bahia de la Vaca Columbus sailed to the eastern tip

Fig.35   From Yamaye (Jamaica) to Española (Haiti)

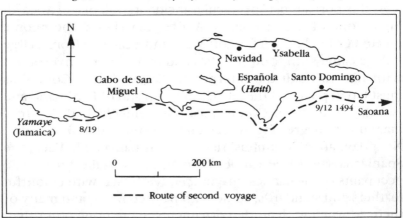

of Jamaica, and named the little headland 'Cabo del Farol', or Cape of the Lighthouse. Of course there could have been no lighthouse there but presumably the villages had fires burning which the Admiral used to guide his vessels around the point. Cabo del Farol is today the site of Morant Bay.

After leaving that cape Columbus did not have to go back to Cuba, and take bearings from there to get to Haiti. Having the exceptional flair of being a seaman who always knew where he was, from the navigational point of view, and moreover, having the advantage of numerous native guides, he set his course north-east-by-east and sailed straight into Haiti at a point he called 'Cabo de San Miguel'. This spot, which is today's Cape Tiburon, Columbus had named after Michele de Cuneo, who was the first to sight land after the fleet had left Jamaica. The date was 19th August and the admiral had taken less than twenty-four hours to cross to Haiti, a distance of about 45 miles.

From there Columbus declined to take the shorter route to Ysabella by steering north-east to Cape San Nicolas then eastwardly for about 200 miles along the north coast. Despite being exhausted, as he must have been, he thought he would take the opportunity to explore Haiti's south coast, for he had not seen this before. There are few records of this journey, which is along a ragged and irregular coastline of about 400 miles, but we see the fleet involved in some ceremony at the eastern tip of Haiti.

The ceremony involved the islet just south of the easterly Haitian peninsula. Again it was the man from the Spanish province of Saona, Michele de Cuneo, who had first spotted the island, and to quote Cuneo, 'Out of love for me the Lord Admiral called it La Bella Saonese. He made me a gift of it and I took possession according to the appropriate modes and forms.' The name 'Saona' has remained.

That was on 12th September 1494. Owing to bad weather and maybe Columbus' exploration of the countryside, the fleet did not set sail from Saona until 24th September.

However, instead of rounding the nearby Cape Engaño to get back to Ysabella, from which he had been away for about four months, the admiral suddenly changed his plans and decided to sail against the Caribs. Therefore the fleet turned south-east to the island of Borinquen, which Columbus had named San Juan Bautista. But within sight of the island a severe fever attacked him, and his officers decided to abandon the expedition and sail with all haste to Ysabella.

At Ysabella, the ailing Christopher Columbus received a dose of heady joy when he saw his brother, Bartholomew, for the first time in about five years. They were very close, these two brothers, and Bartholomew had gone making the rounds of the courts of Europe trying to secure an expedition for his brother, when, unknowing to him, Christopher Columbus found success with Spain. Such was the state of communication in those days that Bartholomew could not have been informed that his brother had sailed. The explorer had written to Bartholomew after his first voyage, and in his letter he asked his brother to hurry to Spain. Yet Bartholomew had not yet reached there before Christopher Columbus left on his second voyage in October 1493.

When Bartholomew Columbus had arrived in Spain he had taken his brother's two sons, Diego and Fernando, to the Spanish court, as had been requested, for the queen had promised to make them pages to the Infante Don Juan. On that occasion Bartholomew had made a great impression on the sovereigns, and when shortly afterwards the ships that the admiral had sent back for urgent provisions reached Spain, the sovereigns, having fitted out the vessels, gave Bartholomew command of the vessels for the journey to Haiti.

Bartholomew had arrived off Ysabella on Midsummer's Day, 1494, before Christopher had returned from his explorations of Cuba, Jamaica, and the south coast of Haiti. Christopher Columbus was overjoyed, and well might this be, for there would be little to cheer him up from hence forward.

A Sea of Troubles

When Christopher Columbus was sailing from Ysabella to explore the south coast of Cuba, so far as his fortunes were concerned he was sailing into a sea of troubles. The amazing thing was that although he had a flair for knowing how things would turn out, and by certain signs in the elements he could accurately forecast the coming of storms, or the appearance of high seas, he seems to have had no intuition whatsoever that the nature of the administration he was leaving behind at Ysabella was very much the setting for sowing the seeds of conflict. Firstly, he had left his brother Diego in charge of Ysabella while he was away, but Diego was certainly too soft to deal with the tough and covetous settlers. Also, he had despatched some of his soldiers into the interior to find gold by any means, and no doubt he guessed what that implied. He had made several other mistakes before leaving to explore Cuba's coastline. There was the case of Alonso de Hojeda who severely punished one of the caciques for what was regarded as the theft of some old clothes. This had alienated all the cacique's people and a great many others besides.

Also, the admiral had sent Mosen Pedro Margarit, one of his roughest and most cruel soldiers, on an armed expedition into the interior with instructions to explore the island and report on its products, at the same time giving him the hollow advice of 'do no harm to the natives'. Margarit's army, or 'gang', – a company of 376 men – had little to exchange for food, but they had to eat, with the result that the most blatant cruelty, thuggery, and pillage took place. Indeed, Columbus, who had not forgotten Caonabó, the cacique held guilty for the murder of the Spaniards at Navidad, had instructed Margarit to capture this cacique. Margarit did not do this but his men apparently went on a wild escapade, extorting food and gold from the natives, and carrying off their wives and daughters, as well as taking many slaves.

This enraged the caciques and Ysabella found itself in a precarious position. Diego Columbus called upon Margarit to mend his ways and this worsened matters because Margarit, who Christopher Columbus had given the authority to do as he thought fit, took serious objection to Diego, and marching on the settlement of Ysabella he seized the three vessels that Bartholomew had brought back, and joined by Fray Buil among others, sailed home to Spain. Fray Buil and Pedro

Margarit were both from the Catalonia province of Spain and always stuck together. But the fact was that the Spaniards as a whole seemed jealous of the Genoese brothers, who, incidentally, by being clannish, did not make things easier for themselves.

Margarit's fleet arrived in Spain in November 1494, and the disgruntled men went to the sovereigns and gave a harsh and bitter account of the Columbus brothers. Columbus heard of the departure of Margarit when he returned from Cuba. Since he was ailing, there was not much he could do. Nevertheless, seeing the chaos, he took the presidency of the Council into his own hands. But things had gone too far. Margarit had left marauding bands, who were so vicious, and who made life so tumultuous for the natives, that it was as if a scourge had befallen that part of Haiti. Yet Christopher Columbus himself was to make things even worse. Instead of punishing the Spanish outlaws for their wrong-doings, he unleashed a reign of terror on the natives. Samuel Eliot Morison in his book *Admiral of the Ocean Sea*, says that the admiral adopted the principle that no Spaniard could do wrong, alleging that 'he held the Indians to strict accountability, sent a force into the interior, hunted down the natives with horses and hounds, rounded up over fifteen hundred of the poor creatures, and brought them back to Ysabella'.

Columbus now wanted to dispose of these people as slaves. He made the suggestion to the sovereigns of Spain in a most vague way, but the sovereigns clearly showed they were not interested. However, the admiral held on to the idea. He had failed to find the much vaunted gold mine of the Cibao that he had talked about, and the hardwoods and other 'precious' material did not prove to be so precious in Spain. He deeply wanted to establish himself as a supplier of slaves from Haiti, and in his view this would cover much of the cost that his expeditions had already incurred.

Some time that autumn the rest of the provision fleet, four caravels under Antonio de Torres, followed the three that Bartholomew Columbus had brought. The fleet of Antonio de Torres made history in that, along with the bringing of provision and other supplies, it brought the first women and children to leave Spain for what was now commonly called '*El Nuevo Mundo*' (The New World). But that was by the way. Now that Christopher Columbus had returned from Cuba and heard about the departure of Margarit he was anxious to have these four vessels return to Spain to enable him to refute at court the lies he knew Margarit was going to tell. At the same opportunity he decided to send 500 of the captured natives of Haiti to the slave mart of Seville.

The admiral went further than that. Of the thousand captives who remained the admiral announced that any of his company could help himself to as many as he wished. When they had done that, the 'rejects' were sent back to their villages.

It is interesting to observe that during all this turmoil and distress for the people of Haiti, Guacanagari remained faithful to Christopher Columbus. This was one of the factors which preserved Columbus and his men from being overwhelmed and wiped out by the natives, for whenever there was conflict, Guacanagari always sent his warriors to help his friend.

Anyway, the cargo of slaves for the slave market of Seville left in the four caravels under the command of Antonio de Torres. The fleet set sail from Ysabella on 24th February 1495, and among the important people on board was Michele de Cuneo, whose accounts have helped so much to inform on what happened during that period, and Christopher Columbus' own brother, Diego. Cuneo tells of the voyage, and among the things we learn is the fate of the 500 slaves. The slaves, confined in hatches below deck, underwent great suffering, especially in stormy weather. Many of them died in mid-ocean, and Cuneo, referring to the last leg of the journey, which was from Madeira to Cadiz, writes: 'About two hundred of these Indians died, I believe, because of the unaccustomed air, colder than theirs. We cast them into the sea. The first land we saw was Cape Spartel, and very soon after we reached Cadiz, in which place we disembarked all the slaves, half of whom were sick'.

Andrés Bernáldez, who said that he saw them on sale at Seville naked as they were born, added: 'They were not very profitable since almost all died, for the country did not agree with them.'

In the midst of the crisis of relationships between the 'men from heaven' and the natives of Haiti, one of the caciques of the Vega Real – a man who had shown great friendship to the Spaniards when they had entered that region for the first time – now decided that the people of Haiti had had enough, and he moved to drive his tormentors into the sea. This cacique, Guatiguana by name, tried to whip up a united front amongst the other caciques, but the rivalries and jealousies which they had always known continued to divide them into hostile camps. Nevertheless, Guatiguana got a considerable army together. Responding to this threat of war from the natives, Christopher Columbus, with such officers as Bartholomew Columbus and Alonso de Hojeda, marched from Ysabella to encounter this army. The Spaniards had 200 foot soldiers, twenty horses, and twenty hounds, and they were assisted by a force of native warriors under Guacanagari. The battle proved to be an anti-climax. In a scene to be repeated again and again throughout the 'Indias' the battle was won by the appearance of horse and rider. Heading the cavalry, Alonso de Hojeda charged into the ranks of his opponents with swinging sword, and the natives, seeing the mounted horsemen, panicked and broke and ran. Why? They imagined that man and beast were one.

Shortly after this victory the Spaniards set out to deal with Caonabó, the cacique whom they alleged had murdered the Spaniards at Navidad. He was also reputed to be the most powerful cacique in the area and an unyielding opponent of the strangers. Columbus wanted him dead or alive, preferably alive.

Caonabó was captured by a simple ruse. Hojeda, with only ten mounted men, went to the Cibao mountains and professed to be visiting Caonabó to invite him to the settlement of Ysabella. Hojeda promised him a treaty of friendship, which also meant protection for him in all his wars. Caonabó agreed to go to Ysabella, but he still took with him an armed force for safety. During the journey Hojeda showed the cacique what looked like burnished bracelets, and told them they were of the kind which were worn on festive occasions by the king of Spain, who was the biggest cacique of all. He said they befitted the dignity of Caonabó and asked would he like to wear them. Of course Caonabó agreed, and the Spaniards slipped them on.

The four glittering bracelets (attached in pairs) that Hojeda had shown Caonabó were in fact handcuffs and foot fetters. After they had been slipped onto Caonabó's hands and feet, the Spaniards fell on the surprised bodyguards and scattered them. Then Caonabó was brought captive to Ysabella.

With Caonabó captured, Christopher Columbus found it much easier to pacify Haiti and the conquistadores succeeded so quickly and easily in breaking the spirit of the native population that soon there was nothing for the strangers to fear. The younger son of the admiral, Ferdinand Columbus, declared that by 1496 the country was so subdued that any lone Spaniard could safely go wherever he pleased, and enjoy 'free food, women, and pick-a-back rides'.

There must have been a considerable loss of the Spanish population of Haiti since 1493, for out of the 1,500 that had sailed with Columbus on his second voyage, the figure given by Ferdinand Columbus regarding the white population of Ysabella in 1495 was 630. Allowing for the fact that some had returned with Margarit, and with Torres, and allowing for the fair number of Spaniards that must have been slain by the natives of Haiti, the mortality rate for the strangers must still have been high.

However, Ysabella was now a well-settled colony and Christopher Columbus felt he could leave it now to return to some pressing matters in Spain. But just then, in June 1495, a hurricane arose and one of the things it did was to sink three ships in Ysabella harbour. The *Niña* was spared, but the admiral lost the *Gallega, Caldera* and *San Juan*. From the wrecks of these a complete little ship, the *Santa Cruz*, was constructed.

From around the middle of 1495 to the end of that year, the Columbus brothers, Diego and Bartholomew, completed the reign of terror on the now frightened people of Haiti. According to Las Casas, forts were built and the Spaniards, now in complete control, marched about the island forcing the people to submit to their rule and exacting tributes of gold from the caciques.

Fig.36   The Spaniards' reign of terror

Paying the tributes of gold that Christopher Columbus exacted was sometimes so difficult that some of the caciques pleaded with him to waive them. But all in vain. In one case Christopher Columbus exacted from the cacique, Manicaotax, a calabash full of gold every three months. But there was not the gold in Haiti to allow for this. Las Casas says that the admiral, so anxious to repay the sovereigns for their great expenditure, would not budge. The people were tortured and persecuted, and if, through revenge, a Spaniard happened to be killed, then not just the killer would pay for it, but the whole population of the village. Their despair was so great that many of them took cassava poison as a way out.

How many, then, of these native people were exterminated during that period? S.E. Morison gives an estimate of the population of Haiti just before Columbus as 300,000, and it is said that no less than 100,000 were wiped out between 1494 and 1496.[2]

In October 1495 Juan Aguado brought a fleet of four caravels from Spain and anchored off Ysabella. Aguado brought supplies and a man skilled in metals, for which Columbus had asked, so this was good news. But the bad news was that Aguado, who had returned to Spain with Antonio Torres, had been sent by the sovereigns of Spain to conduct an enquiry into Columbus' conduct as Viceroy and Governor. This was of course the follow-up to the complaints of Margarit and Fray Buil. Aguado, who it is reported, made a pompous and triumphant entry into Ysabella, did not find Columbus there, for the admiral was on an expedition in the interior. He appeared to take control as a result, assuming the functions of viceroy. Bartholomew Columbus, upset, sent word to his brother, who returned to Ysabella forthwith, but who was full of courtesy towards Juan Aguado.

As Aguado continued his enquiries, taking abundant testimony from colonists, most of whom were discontented, Columbus began to feel it was time he went back home to look after his interests. He wanted to do this before Aguado's report was sent in, since he feared the worst.

Meanwhile, the Spanish officials were very dissatisfied about the site of Ysabella, and one of the main reasons for this was because its position offered no protection from the north winds. Columbus sent out an exploring party under Miguel Diaz, and Diaz alighted on a site that he considered excellent for building a city. It had a good harbour, attractive terrain, land reputed to be fertile for agriculture, and rivers which were

2   By 1512 only 20,000 of these Arawak peoples were alive, and by 1548 Oviedo thought there might be less than 500 in existence.

supposed to be gold-bearing.

Christopher Columbus left for Spain in March 1496, but before he left he gave instructions to his brother Bartholomew to found the new city. Bartholomew started the building of the new city either in that very year, 1496, or early in 1497. He called the city 'Santo Domingo'. Ysabella, the first city ever to be built in the so-called 'New World', and up to that time the capital of the Spanish 'Indias', was abandoned.

Homeward Again

Christopher Columbus quietly and unimpressively set sail for Spain with a fleet of two ships – the *Santa Clara* (formerly the *Niña*) and the *Santa Cruz* (nicknamed the *India*), the first ship to be constructed in this part of the world. So many people had been disillusioned and eager to go home that both ships were overcrowded on the passage to Spain. The ships were carrying 225 Spaniards and thirty of the native people. Among the thirty was Caonabó, who died at sea.

Whether it was because of the overcrowding of the ship is not known, but the course Columbus took, in relation to winds and currents, was a very slow one indeed. He appeared to head south-east by east, making extremely slow progress, and soon food and water were running so short that they made for the nearest land, which happened to be Maria Galante, the first land the admiral had seen when he had arrived in the 'Indias' at the beginning of this second voyage. Indeed, it seemed that steering this way was deliberate, but Columbus does not say this. Next morning the two ships sailed for Guadeloupe, and Columbus sent an armed boat ashore. Warrior women appeared from the forests and attacked them. Columbus sent some of the 'Indians' who he had aboard to make peace. Later, they again fell into an ambush, this time from a group of men who resisted their landing, but the warriors were routed by Spanish arms. After that the Spaniards went into the village, looted and destroyed their huts, giving the impression to the people of this land, Kerukera, that this white tribe was not only the most powerful, but the most bestial they had seen.

But that was not all. A party of armed Spaniards pursued their adversaries into the mountains and managed to capture about a dozen people, among whom was a lady cacique. Holding these as hostage the Spaniards were able to obtain provisions. Among the things they relished was cassava bread, which the women of the island taught them how to make with the abundant cassava roots which they sold them.

Columbus and his seamen must have liked Guadeloupe a great deal for on this occasion they remained there nine days. During this time it is reported they did much baking of cassava bread. When they finally left Guadeloupe, they released all the hostages, except the lady cacique and her daughter, whom they took with them on the voyage home.

Once again the fleet found itself in a sea of troubles. The fact that the ships were so crowded meant that whatever food they had on board was in danger of being consumed quickly. What made it worse was that it was going to be a long voyage, for the caravels did not have the wind in their favour to make good progress. Ferdinand Columbus, then eight years old, (and who was not there) later wrote that the food situation was so acute that the ships' company was put on a daily allowance of six ounces of cassava bread and a little cup of water. He further says: 'And although there were eight or nine pilots aboard these two caravels none of them knew where they were but the admiral was confident that their position lay somewhat to the westward of the Azores'.

In the end Columbus displayed his amazing skill in navigation. He arrived at the coast of Portugal just a short distance from Cabo San Vicente, (Cape St Vincent) at which he had been aiming. Heading for the port of Cadiz, from which he had sailed, the admiral reached it on 11th June 1496 – three months after leaving Ysabella, and three years after leaving Spain on this second voyage.

Was it going to be a period of rest now for the admiral? It promised to be a period of some physical rest but great spiritual unrest. Yet the call of the 'Indias' would come again.

CHAPTER FOUR
The Third Voyage

When Columbus arrived in Spain after the second voyage he had no way of knowing to what extent the sovereigns had been influenced by his many detractors, especially by those who had returned with Margarit, and so he must have waited nervously after word got to them that he had arrived.

Imagine his pleasure, then, when sometime in July words of congratulations from Ferdinand and Isabella reached him, telling him of the pleasure they felt due to his safe return. They asked that he should come to visit them as soon as he could do so, adding, 'since in what has passed you have had much hardship'.

Columbus must have been overjoyed and eager to be in the royal presence again. But it was not easy to get there because at this time the Spanish court was at Almazán, about 100 miles north of Madrid. However, Columbus planned to undertake the journey, and this not only to see Ferdinand and Isabella, but to restore his badly tarnished reputation with the people. As we have seen, at the outset of the second voyage there was great jubilation and great enthusiasm for Spain's 'New World', and about the prospect of riches for Spain because of promise of gold and other abundant wealth of the 'Indias'. Columbus, who was responsible for this brilliant prospect, was the great hero. But with the many reversals he had had in the period of the second voyage (1493 to 1496), leading to the rushing back to Spain of his adversaries to spread ill reports of him, along with the tales of cruelty, and chaos and confusion in what had been a paradise – because of these things the people's admiration for Christopher Columbus had diminished sharply. In 1493 the ordinary man in the street had railed and clamoured to go with Columbus on the second voyage, but

Fig.37 Isabella of Spain

there had hardly been room for him. The well-born and the
well-landed had largely kept him out. Now nobody wanted
to go. The masses had been led to believe among other things,
that going to the 'Indias' was a waste of time, and that in any

case there was little gold to be found in those parts.

Therefore the 'Admiral of the Ocean Sea' intended to make of the journey from Seville (where he stayed) to Almazán, a march of triumph. He had with him two close relatives of the cacique Caonabó – a nephew and a brother. Whenever the group was about to enter a town Caonabó's brother would wear around his neck a beautiful collar with links of heavy gold. According to Andrés Bernáldez, who said he held this gold collar in his hands, they displayed many other things that were used by the people of the 'Indias', such as crowns, masks, and woven articles of cotton. Coincidentally, as Christopher Columbus was on his way to Almazán, the Spanish court was moving to Burgos, about 50 miles away to the north-west. The admiral changed route and hurried there for, apart from wishing to see the sovereigns, he was most anxious to see his young sons, who were pages to the Infante Don Juan.[1] Diego Columbus was almost a young man now, for he was about sixteen, while Ferdinand was eight. Columbus arrived at the court even before the sovereigns. The sovereigns reached Burgos a few days later and greeted Columbus warmly, which went a long way to assure him that the many complaints made against him held no weight so far as they were concerned. He felt happy to be in their presence, and they were full of praise and goodwill for him, and promised to compensate him for all his troubles.

He presented Ferdinand and Isabella not only with the ornaments he had brought to display on the journey but with the two 'Indians': Caonabó's brother, who was baptized as 'Don Diego', and the nephew.

Christopher Columbus, who had resolved on making a third voyage to the 'Indias', thought it an excellent time to put his case. He asked for eight ships, two to head directly for Española, and six to venture on an expedition to find the mainland. Although the sovereigns smiled and said he would have exactly what he wished, there were a number of other things to do and not much money to do them with, and so

1   Infante or infant heir to the throne. Don Juan was the child of Ferdinand and Isabella.

it took two whole years before the admiral found himself again on the ocean sea.

The Voyage

Columbus set sail from the Mediterranean port of San Lucar de Barrameda on 30th May 1498. His fleet consisted of six ships. This voyage was going to be different from the other two. For he had not found the gold that Marco Polo had written about, nor had he found the palace of the Great Khan. This had worried him and he had re-examined a theory by the Portuguese King Dom João II that a great continent lay astride the Equator somewhere in the western seas. Not only was a great continent to be found but in that land there would be an abundance of gold and spices.

Columbus also felt that there might be other islands south of Maria Galante, the first landfall he had made on his second voyage. In fact, it is almost certain that he was told this by his 'Indian' guides. But discovering whether this was really true or not was of secondary importance. Just before he set sail he went to church, as was his custom, to ask for special blessings and protection for the voyage, and this, the third voyage, he dedicated to 'the Three Persons in One God', the Blessed Trinity. And as usual he made a vow. This time he vowed that the first land he encountered he would name after the Blessed Trinity.[2].

It is not certain how many people he had with him, since his journal of this voyage is lost. But we know that among the company was the Italian, Amerigo Vespucci[3], there was Bartholomew de las Casas, and Alonso de Hojeda – three men later to become prominent in the affairs of the 'Indias'.

As Christopher Columbus sailed from San Lucar, there was a danger not too far away. Spain was at war with France at that time and a French fleet was lying in wait for him off Cape St Vincent (Cabo San Vicente), the south-westerly tip of

---

2 Thus *Trinidad*, which is Trinity in English.
3 Amerigo who gave his name to America.

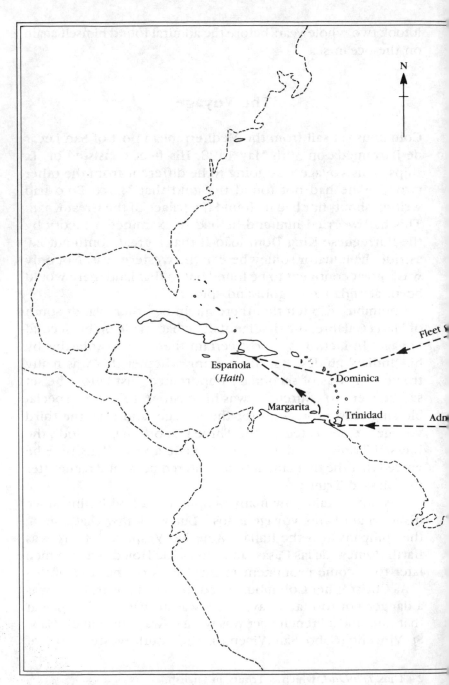

Fig.38   The course of Columbus' third voyage

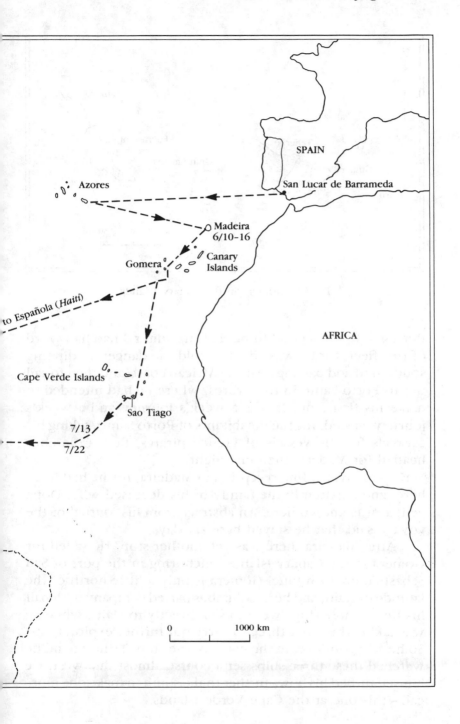

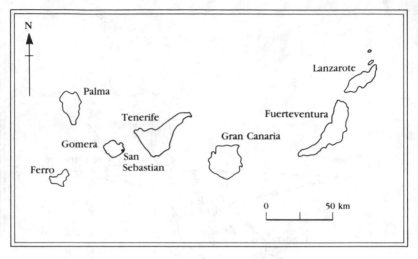

Fig.39   Gomera in the Canary Islands

Portugal. It was a good thing that the admiral had had word of this fleet, for he was able to avoid the danger by dipping southward and passing near the African coast, and then to sail out to Porto Santo in the Azores, where he had intended to make his first stop. It was a week's journey and a week's journey wasted, for the inhabitants of Porto Santo, taking his caravels for the vessels of French pirates, fled. Columbus headed for Madeira the same night.

He was given a fine reception in Madeira, for he had lived here, and apparently the family of his deceased wife, Dona Felipa, was known here. An abstract from his journal of the voyage said that he stayed here six days.

After Madeira there was yet another stop. He sailed for Gomera in the Canary Islands, anchoring in the port of San Sebastian on 19th June. Gomera is only a little north of the latitude of Haiti, and here Columbus parted company with half his fleet. Three ships were to sail directly to Haiti, while he was taking the other three to carry out further explorations. So he said goodbye 'in the name of the Holy Trinity', and he watched these three ships set a course almost due west. He himself turned his bows further to the south to make one more call – this one at the Cape Verde Islands.

Columbus had planned to reach as far south as this point, the Cape Verde Islands having a latitude not far north of the Equator, and it was the Admiral's intention to steer westerly from here, gradually bearing to the south to see if he could arrive at the mainland that Dom João II had spoken about.

He appears to have delayed in the Cape Verde Islands, going from harbour to harbour, isle to isle, stocking up on some salted goats' meat, and listening to all sorts of legends about lands beyond the waves – he was never tired of this subject. Maybe there was something in particular he wanted to hear from these old seamen. He did not set sail from the Cape Verde Islands until 4th July in that year 1498.

Now it was open sea. There were to be no more stops until he reached the 'Indias' or, as he hoped, Dom João's land.

Sailing south-west from São Tiago in the Cape Verde Islands Columbus reached the region of calm called the Doldrums, around 13th July. The seamen were on the point of panicking, for it was not only calm but they found the temperature unbearably hot. They had never been so far south before and legendary stories about being consumed by the heat of the

Fig.40   The Cape Verde Islands

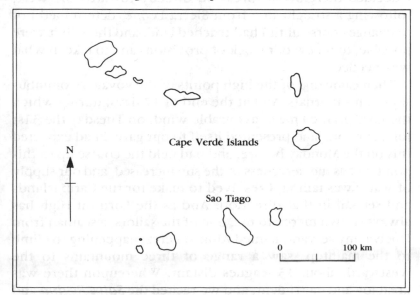

Equator seemed to scare them. The admiral says in his journal, 'The wind stopped so suddenly and unexpectedly, and the heat was so excessive and immoderate, that there was no one who dared to go below to look after the casks of wine and water, which burst, snapping the hoops of the pipes. The wheat burned like fire; the bacon and salted meat roasted and putrified.' It is useful to quote this if only to show how easily the admiral could let his imagination run away with him. Was it fear that led him or his seamen to see such things? Or was it Columbus' tendency to exaggerate? Could the wheat really have been burning like fire? As he sails into the west we shall have more reason to examine some of his other statements.

His journal says that the heat lasted eight days, the first day of which was sunny, and the rest overcast. But on the following day, 22nd July, his fortunes changed completely. A great wind arose and filled his sails, and the little fleet sped along. He was averaging as many as 183 miles a day, and at this point he changed course. He wrote in his log: 'I decided to go due west. I steered towards the west, not venturing to go any further southward, because I noticed a great change in the sky and in the stars, although I found no change in the temperature. I decided therefore to press on directly towards the west, following a straight line from Sierra Leone, determined not to change course until I had reached land, and there, if it were possible, to renew our stock of provisions and to take in what was needed.'

Then came one of the high points of the voyage. Columbus says in his journal: 'And at the end of 17 days, during which the Lord granted me a favourable wind, on Tuesday the 31st July, at noon, land presented itself to our gaze. I had expected this on the Monday before, and had held the course up to this point, but as the fierceness of the sun increased, and our supply of water was failing, I resolved to make for the Carib islands and set sail in that direction. And as the Lord on High has always shown mercy to me, one of the sailors, a seaman from Huelva, my servant, named Alonso Pérez, happening to climb to the maintop, saw a range of three mountains to the westward, about 15 leagues distant. Whereupon there was great joy and merriment, and we recited the *Salve Regina* and gave thanks to the Lord.'[4]

The admiral continued, 'I then abandoned the northward course and turned towards the land . . . We reached a cape which I called Cape Galea – I had already called the island "Trinidad" – and Cape Galea would have been an excellent harbour if it were deep. There we saw houses and people and very fair lands, lands as beautiful and green as the gardens of Valencia in the month of March.'

There is no reason to doubt that the look-out saw a range of three mountains to the westward, but those mountains were bound to be mountains of the Northern Range, since there is no 'range of three mountains' elsewhere in Trinidad, and certainly not in the region misleadingly called 'Trinity', where the non-existent Trinity Hills are supposed to be situated. This is at Guayaguayare where the admiral approached the land. The look-out, Alonso Pérez of Huelva, saw the mountains from 15 leagues (about 45 miles) away and it is certain that at that distance he would have seen only the highest peaks of the island, and these are in the Northern Range. The difficulty is, however, that there are no three well-defined peaks to be seen even there and one wonders if the vision of Alonso Pérez was aided by clouds in the distance, or if, knowing of Columbus' vow to name the first land he saw after the Trinity, Pérez mischievously took a leaf from the admiral's own book, telling the admiral what he would have liked to hear.

However, if Columbus could not be blamed for this misconception, he must certainly be taken to task for one of the statements he makes in the above passage. It is this: 'There we saw houses and people and very fair lands, lands as beautiful and green as the gardens of Valencia in the month of March.' If some time had elapsed between the event of the encounter with Trinidad and Columbus' writing about it in his log then maybe Columbus may have been confusing Trinidad with some of the places he visited afterwards. The admiral could not have seen houses or huts in the vicinity of Point Galeota in 1498, for the reason that none existed.

---

4   The 17 days Columbus referred to was after leaving the Cape Verde Islands, but it was 63 days after leaving Spain.

It is absolutely certain that he saw no people on that occasion, for he himself tells of an incident, days later, when he saw the inhabitants of the island for the first time.

Then why did Columbus make this entry in his log? The student of the voyages of Columbus would find him making these beautiful-sounding and extravagant remarks often, and would probably know why. It was Columbus' attempt to keep the sovereigns of Spain interested and impressed. for he had already made two voyages and had as yet found no gold to speak of, and the sovereigns, against the wishes of their advisers, had persisted with him, investing large sums of money – money that Spain could ill-afford – to send him on these voyages. Also, by the third voyage, he had made many enemies, as we have seen, and it was only the sovereigns' continued faith in him that kept him sailing.

Columbus came in to Cape Galea 'at the hour of complines', which would be at about six o'clock in the evening. He does not speak about mountains now, of course, because there are none in sight. He was unable to stay in Cape Galea because, as he said, the harbour was not deep enough for anchorage. Incidentally, he declared that he called the cape 'Galea', because it looked like a galley under sail. However, a later Spanish map-maker wrote down 'Galeota' on that part of the map – the south-eastern point – and on the north-eastern point he wrote 'Galera'[5].

Easing along at Cape Galea, and really not having any great desire to land, the Admiral sailed along the south coast, in that channel which now bears his name. The next day, Wednesday 1st August 1498, he anchored at a point he called 'Punta de la Playa', literally 'Point of the Beach'. This is most likely to be what we know today as Moruga Beach. It appears that he anchored here because he spotted the river, which flowed just beside the point or headland. He sent men ashore to fill casks of water, for they were desperate for drinking water, and of course the men would have been glad to stretch their legs. They saw not a single inhabitant, but they noticed certain animal footprints which they thought to be of goats, but which

5   Both Galeota and Galea are kinds of galley.

were probably deer. They also found some fishing implements.

After getting back to the ship, Columbus continued his journey along the coast. Just at this time, due south of him, he began seeing a coastline in the haze of distance. It was the mainland, or course, the mainland for which he was searching, but he did not know this. Deeming this to be another of the many islands in these seas, he named it 'La Isla Santa', or Holy Island.

The next day, Thursday 2nd August 1498, Columbus' fleet reached the south-western tip of the island he called Trinidad and anchored. He named the place 'Punta del Arenal' or 'Sandy Point'. It was here, according to his log, that he saw the inhabitants of the island for the very first time.

It is almost beyond doubt that ever since the 'Admiral of the Ocean Sea' had reached the island, eyes had been peering in disbelief at the three big canoes with the great sheets fluttering in the wind. He had named the land after the Holy Trinity, perhaps not even caring to know what it was called by the inhabitants. The inhabitants called it 'Kairi' or 'Iëre' which, in the Arawak dialect of these parts, meant 'the island just next to the continent'. The few native guides he had with him seemed to have been as much strangers here as he was. They may never have ventured so far south.

It was quite clear from the way the admiral was skirting the coast that he had no intention of coming ashore at Kairi. Having already abandoned all plans to search for the land Dom João II had written about, his thoughts were already on his settlement on the island of Haiti, the land he called Española. He had given orders to abandon the settlement of Ysabella and to found the new settlement on the south coast of the island, but that was two years ago and he had not yet seen the new town. And then there were many other things for him to attend to over there. He simply was not going to delay long at Kairi, the land he called Trinidad.

But seeing inhabitants now sharpened his interest. His ships were lying at anchor when a canoe containing twenty-four men put off from the shore. They came towards the ships, then stopped a short distance off, and shouted to the Spaniards. They may have been trying to ask what manner of men were the strangers and from whence they had come. Not strangely, Columbus said he could not understand a single word they said, nor could they understand him. He said that he motioned them to draw nearer but they did not move. He wrote in his log: 'Wishing to attract them so that they would come nearer, I ordered the ship's tambourine to be beaten and the boys to perform a national dance.'

But the men in the canoe mistook the national dance for a war-dance and let fly a shower of arrows. The Spaniards, riled, hit back with crossbows, and the Arawaks took flight. The canoe was soon on shore. But the rowers came back in the end for they were eager to know who were these people – this white-skinned tribe with their bodies covered with animal skin (or maybe worked cotton), and with only head and arms exposed, and with those great canoes that needed no oars! They tried to talk with the Spaniards and after a long and difficult parley, with neither side understanding the other, the quarrel appeared to have been patched up. There are different versions as to what happened after this moment. Bartholomew de las Casas, a friend and confidante of Columbus, and who was in possession of all the Columbus' diaries, and moreover a man who was on the spot at the time, described how a cacique went aboard Columbus' flagship, the *Vaqueños*, and how he placed a golden crown on Columbus' head, and how Columbus placed a red cap on his. The story is colourful but most likely to be untrue. Las Casas was recalling this after he had seen many other such ceremonies. There was never much gold in this island of Kairi, or Trinidad, and the natives never seemed to set much store by the metal. What is recorded is that the Spaniards were invited to land. Columbus himself did not leave the ship, and it seemed he was suffering from the arthritis which had attacked him severely at the end of his second voyage. Not much is known about the meeting on shore, but it was said to have been friendly. There is a pleasant picture of an exchange of gifts, but again no reliable records. The Spaniards were described as taking water here also, this time by sinking wells in the sand.

The Spaniards had a good impression of the people of Kairi – or at least of the people they saw. These people were not as completely naked as those in other parts, and in some ways they seemed quite advanced. Columbus described them as handsome and well-formed and wearing worked cotton about their loins, as well as gaily-coloured bandannas around their foreheads. In addition to their bows and arrows they carried square shields, and this intrigued Columbus, for he said he had seen nothing like this before anywhere in the 'Indias'.

That night Columbus became very disturbed about the current outside of Punta del Arenal. In a letter intended for Ferdinand and Isabella, he said: 'I anchored there, under the said Punta del Arenal, outside of the strait, and found the water rushing from east to west with such fury, and this continued all the time, so that it appeared impossible to move backwards for the current, or to move forward for the shoals. At the dead of night, while I was on deck, I heard an awesome roaring that came from the south towards the ships. I stopped to observe what it might be, and I saw the sea rolling from west to east like a mountain as high as the ship, and approaching slowly. On top of this rolling sea came a mighty wave, and in all this uproar there were other conflicting currents producing the sound of breakers upon the rocks. To this day I have a vivid recollection of the dread I felt lest the ship should founder against the force of that tremendous sea.'

But nothing much happened except that the Admiral's flagship lost an anchor.[6]

This happened on the Thursday, and the next day, Friday 3rd August 1498, Columbus sent men to test the depth of the strait, and they found it to be seven fathoms – a most satisfactory depth. He wrote: 'It pleased God to give me a favourable wind, and I passed through the middle of the strait, after which I regained my tranquillity.' Deeming the strait to be treacherous and full of dangers he named it 'Boca de la Sierpe' or 'The Serpent's Mouth'.

As Columbus entered the gulf, sailing due north from Punta del Arenal, and thinking of a northern passage to get quickly back to Haiti, he noticed, along the coast which dipped in to

6   An anchor, believed to be the one lost by Columbus that night, was found on Constant Estate, Cedros, in 1877.

the east, a piece of land jutting out, with the surface jagged
and resembling a cock's spur. He called this little headland
'El Gallo' or 'The Cock'. Shortly afterwards, as the ships were
moving up through the waters, a whale surfaced and spouted,
and Columbus called the water 'Golfo de la Ballena' or 'Gulf
of the Whale'. As he sailed he was watching the coastline some
distance to the west of him, and thinking it to be another
island, he admired the graceful mountains and named the land
'Isla de Gracia'. He reached the northern passage and this
looked even more menacing than the one in the south. Huge,
forbidding mountains lay on either hand, and the passage itself
was all but barred by three islets, and no doubt by hidden
rocks. He turned away hoping there was somewhere else to
pass. But, despite the anxiety about the western passage, and
his thoughts of getting back to Haiti, he was still thinking of
the treasures he had not found. For he could write: 'Up to
now I have had no speech with the people of these lands, and
I really desired it, so I turned towards the Island of Gracia.'

He went to that shore and some of his men landed, and
when they came back telling Columbus that they saw gold,
Columbus immediately left the ship and rowed to land. Here
he must have had the happiest time of the entire third voyage.
On shore he met a cacique who must have reminded him of
Guacanagari in Haiti, for the cacique received him most
warmly, and took him inland to his own house and entertained
him, and offered him great friendship. He saw gold being used
as if it were of no value, and he received many gifts of it. He
enquired about the mines that the gold came from but the
cacique, who was willing to take him there, told him that the
mines were several days' journey away. Columbus said he was
pressed, he could not go now, but that he would come back
soon. He observed the wife of the cacique wearing pearls, and
he was very interested and anxious to get some, and he was
told there was an island to the north of where they were where
people dived for them. He asked the exact location.

Columbus did not want to delay much more. He was anxious
to find a passage and get the wind in his sails and ride the
waves to Haiti. The cacique had told Columbus that the land
where they were was called Paria and that it was part of the

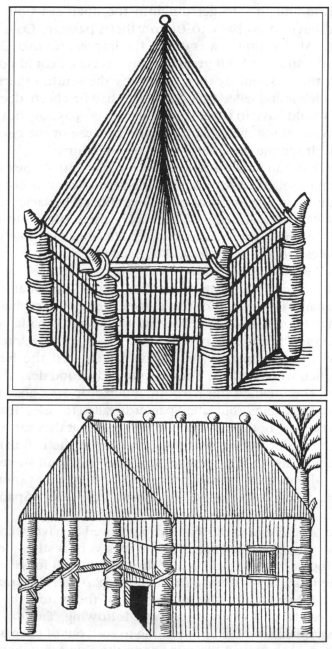

Fig.41   Types of Indian houses from Oviedo's
La hystoria generale de las Indias, 1547

mainland and that to get out into the open sea Columbus would have to go back to the northern passage. Columbus wrote: 'At that time I was under the impression that Gracia was an island . . . I felt great anxiety because I could not get out by the west nor by the east nor by the south. I therefore lifted anchor and sailed back to where I had first been, deciding that I would have to leave by the northwest passage, but I did not return along the inhabited parts because of the currents which drove me completely out of my course.'

The days had flown by and it was Sunday 12th August when Columbus sailed back to the northern passage. It is not clear why this great seafarer was so nervous about this placid, almost land-locked sea. In front of him were three islets and there might have been fierce currents. He pulled into a harbour in the most westerly of the islets, and noticed that the place was full of monkeys. He called the harbour 'Puerto de Gatos', or 'Port of Cats'. The isle itself he named 'El Caracol', the Spanish for 'The Snail'. The natives of this place called it 'Chacachacare', a name that is said to represent the sounds made by its monkeys. On another nearby islet – an islet he named 'El Delfin' (The Dolphin) – the Spaniards entered the huts of fishermen who had fled. They also found a good deal of fresh water. They named the harbour 'Puerto de las Cabanas' or 'Port of the Cabins', but later Spaniards called the islet 'Huevos' (eggs) because of the number of birds' eggs that they saw there. The third islet, which was the one nearest the mainland of Kairi, was also full of monkeys. It was an island so regular and without inlets, in other words, so blunt, that Columbus said he called it 'Cabo Boto' or 'Blunt Cape'. Later Spaniards simply called it 'Monos', because of its monkeys.

The 'Admiral of the Ocean Sea' appeared to have been very uneasy among these islets. For he was very restive; he was growing desperate to get out of the gulf and sail for Haiti. He decided to take his chance through the passage. He remained for a while watching the movement of the waters, his sails at the ready, and when, on the day following, Tuesday 14th August, he noticed the tide seeming to rush out of the passage, he lifted anchor, and his ships rode the tide safely between the rocks, and he was out into the open sea. Great was his

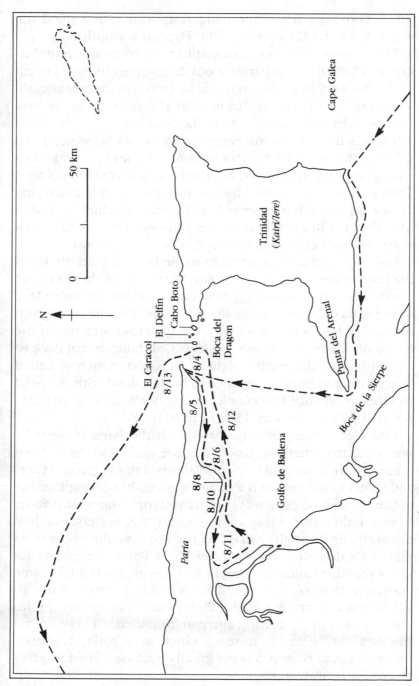

Fig.42 Explorations round Trinidad to Paria and Boca del Dragon

relief. Looking back at the dangerous waters he named the place 'Boca del Dragon' or 'The Dragon's Mouth'.

Then comes a strange statement in the journal. Columbus says that he sighted an island about 26 leagues (78 miles) north of the Boca del Dragon – an island he calls 'Isla de la Asuncion' – and he goes on to say that from the same place he saw another which he calls, 'Isla de la Concepcion'.

The Isla de la Asuncion is obviously Grenada, which is 70 miles to the north of the Dragon's Mouth, and mountainous enough to be seen from Trinidad on a clear day. Mountainous Tobago, too, was spotted by the admiral who recorded that he saw an island lying towards the east, and which he called 'Bellaforma'. Regarding Isla de la Concepcion, one historian says: 'La Concepcion, I imagine, was only a cloud.'

Columbus did not sail north from the Dragon's Mouth. From the time he left the Dragon's Mouth he set his course somewhat north-westerly then swung down towards the northern face of the Paria coastline, for he did not forget the direction given to him by the friendly cacique as to the exact location of the island of pearls. Yet so anxious was Columbus to get back to the settlement that within sight of an island, which he called 'Margarita' and which happened to be the island with the pearl fisheries, he changed his course, swung north again and headed for Haiti. The date was 15th August 1498.

Although when Columbus was with the Paria cacique he was told that where he stood was the mainland, he did not quite believe it. He had been told similar tales regarding Cuba and Haiti by caciques on the earlier voyages but his exploration of the coasts of these lands had proved their statements false. It was either that these caciques did not understand him properly, or through conceit wanted to give the impression that their domains were limitless. But Bartholomew de las Casas says that Columbus, just before leaving for Haiti, became conscious that so great a land as he had just seen was not an island but a continent. Columbus himself, as quoted by las Casas, makes the following entry in his journal: 'I believe that this is a very great continent, which until today has been unknown. And reason aids me greatly because of that so great river and fresh-water sea.'

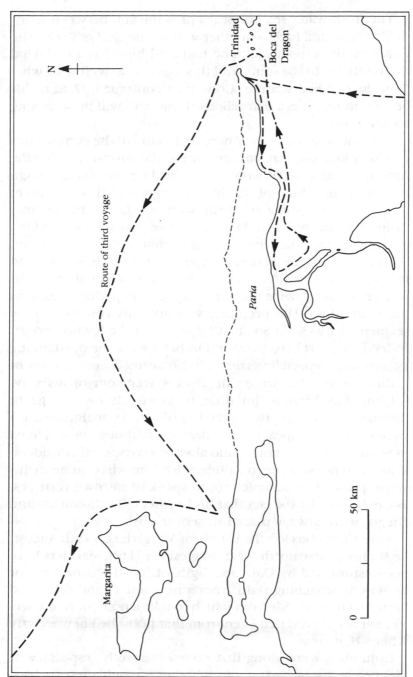

Fig. 43 Margarita, the island of pearls

The fresh-water sea he speaks of is the gulf between Kairi, or Trinidad, and Paria – in other words, the Gulf of Paria. The Carib captives in Guadeloupe had told him that a mainland definitely lay to the south and this meshed so well with what Dom João II had written. Columbus continued: 'And if this be a continent it is a marvellous thing, and will be so among all the wise . . .'

It might be as well to say here that many of the companions of Columbus on that voyage – men like Alonso de Hojeda, Amerigo Vespucci, Peralonso Niño, and Hernan Pérez, sought to claim the glory of having 'discovered' this continent for Spain, and some of them went so far as to say that Columbus never even landed. Quite apart from seeking personal fame, they never forgot that Columbus was no Spaniard, but a Genoese sailing for Spain. All these men had felt secretly resentful about this, for it seemed that this foreigner was showing them the way (except perhaps Vespucci the Florentine). This prejudice was not only confined to the seamen. It was so in Spain at large and at the Spanish court. Indeed, at court Ferdinand and Isabella were the outstanding exceptions, especially Isabella, who seemed deeply fond of Columbus and for whom he always went out of his way.

Columbus himself did little to ward off the charge of 'foreigner'. He was always talking of Genoa, maintained his Genoese ways of speaking and dressing (although he had lived in Spain for several years), and always gave special consideration to Genoese seamen sailing with him – like some of his ships' pilots, for example, not to speak of his own relatives, as can be seen by the fact that his brothers, Bartholomew and Diego, were always placed in senior positions.

After Columbus left the waters of Margarita on 15th August, he set his course north-west-by-west for Haiti. Mariners have been astonished by Columbus' gift of 'dead-reckoning', for he was approaching Haiti from a new angle, and there had been no known lands from which to take a point of reference. Yet events proved that even from that point he knew exactly where Haiti was.

Columbus went along that course carefully, especially at night-time, for he had no idea whether it would be as studded

Fig.44   A 16th-century compass card

with islands as was the case on the second voyage when he touched at Maria Galante. After four days sailing, just before nightfall on 19th August, they came within sight of land. He encountered and named two little islets off Haiti – one which he had seen before and which he now called 'Beata' after a virgin, and the other, which looked like a sail from afar, he called 'Alto Velo', meaning 'High Sail'.

Then came a touching moment. The three caravels that had sailed directly to Haiti from Ferro in the Canary Islands had been spotted from Santo Domingo passing to leeward, and Bartholomew Columbus, thinking his brother was aboard, had set sail to catch them. He did not, but on 21st August he met Christopher at Beata. It was a joyful meeting, for Christopher Columbus and his brothers were always very close, and they had not seen each other for almost two and a half years. There was a lot of bad news to report, but that could wait.

The 'Admiral of the Ocean Sea' and his caravels left Beata on 22nd August, and the vessels anchored in the port of Santo Domingo on 31st August, in that year 1498.

Columbus at Santo Domingo

When Columbus arrived in Santo Domingo he found the settlement and the country in the worst possible situation he could have imagined. It stemmed in some measure from the incident in June 1496 when Columbus had encountered in the port of Cadiz three vessels that were poised to set sail for Ysabella. Columbus had sent a letter by the captain of that fleet, Peralonsa Niño, to his brother Bartholomew, who was in charge of the settlement, stating that the slave trade could continue, providing that the slaves were genuine prisoners of war. This was of course Christopher's own decision, for he had only just reached Cadiz. In any case the Spanish sovereigns – especially Isabella – had always been against any trading in slaves. On receipt of Christopher's letter Bartholomew Columbus had promptly got hold of 300 'Indians' to send to the slave markets of Cadiz and Seville by means of Niño's fleet. The question about genuine prisoners of war did not arise because Bartholomew simply had to state they were prisoners of war, and in fact it would not have really mattered how he got them. And Christopher Columbus knew that well. In any case the Spaniards in Haiti were making raids all the time, for no other purpose but looting and plundering, and particularly for taking prisoners. So Bartholomew, who was the *Adelantado*, the highest ranking officer, and acting Governor, must have drawn the wrath of other high-ranking officers, who, knowing that the Spanish crown was against the slave trade, must have felt that these two Genoese were acting as they liked and filling their pockets with the profits. Rebellion had been already seething, just months after the admiral had left Ysabella.

Just before this time there came a story-like interlude. It told of what amounted to a state visit by Bartholomew Columbus to the cacique Behechio of the province of Xaragua in south-western Haiti. Powerful cacique though Behechio was, the caciques of Haiti were all conscious of the vast superiority of the invaders in terms of battle strategy, arms, and fire-power, and they were all seeking to cultivate their friendship and goodwill as a protection against their enemies, and indeed as an ally to aid their future conquests. Despite the brutal treatment that they and their subjects were all receiving from the Spaniards they were so divided among themselves, and each so wishing the upperhand against the others, that they were always seeking to cajole and pander to the very enemies who were seeking to eliminate them. In fact all the historians commenting on that period agree that the Spaniards, despite their force of arms, could have been driven into the sea in one night had all the caciques of Haiti combined against them. For at that stage the Spaniards did not number more than one thousand, a tiny figure when compared to the several thousands of 'Indians' who surrounded them.

The interlude which was so much like a fairy-tale, brightened that period. Bartholomew de las Casas, who, as was said, was on the voyage, and who, later, was the beneficiary of so much of the Columbian papers, gives a picture of what transpired on the occasion. Bartholomew Columbus and his soldiers, in full and no doubt ceremonial armour, marched through forests studded with immortelles, crossed the River Yaque, met Behechio on the border of his territory, and were conducted by him to his resplendent residence in the beautiful and green territory around a lake the strangers named 'Enriquillo'. The visitors were met there by a cortège of Behechio's wives, and were entertained for three days. The highlights of the visit were sumptuous iguana feasts, mock battles, and lively dancing by maidens waving palm branches. To close, at the end of the third day, Behechio's sister, Anacaona, who had been the wife of Caonabó, was brought in on a litter dressed only in flowers. Bartholomew Columbus was so delighted with the grand display that he did not bother to exact the normal tribute of gold that the caciques had to pay to the Spaniards, but instead accepted payment in hemp, cotton and cassava.

However, Bartholomew could not have been so delighted when he returned to Santo Domingo. He walked straight into trouble – a rebellion engineered, ironically enough, by his *Alcalde Mayor*, or Chief Justice, Francisco Roldán. Roldán, who, like most of the other Spaniards, had an insatiable greed for gold, had long resented the fact that all the tributes of gold was reserved to the Crown. Officially, that was, for he suspected that the two 'foreigners' – the Columbus brothers – were secretly enriching themselves. The question of despatching 300 slaves to be sold in Spain was also seen as a private deal of the Columbus brothers. On top of all this,

Roldán must have thought Bartholomew was making a triumphant visit to Xaragua, where he would receive royal treatment and exact his rich tribute of gold.

The Chief Justice had already been trying to undermine Bartholomew Columbus' authority by promising the caciques, through his supporters, that he was going to relieve them of having to pay tributes of gold. This was bound to be great news, for not many of them could easily raise the amount of gold exacted. To get support from his fellow Spaniards he promised them a life of ease with abundant natives to dig up any amount of gold for them. He promised to abolish taxes, and a free passage home to Spain for those who wished to go back. Feeling sure of support in Haiti because of these secret promises, and counting on the anti-Columbus faction who had returned to Spain to secure the abolition of Christopher Columbus' privilege, he set to bring about what looked like the first political revolt in the 'New World', at least, the first to be recorded.

Bartholomew Columbus and Francisco Roldán had actually confronted each other when the advanced fleet of the third voyage arrived at Santo Domingo. News that the sovereigns of Spain had confirmed Columbus' privilege was a great psychological blow to Roldán, and now his fight seemed pointless. Fighting against Christopher Columbus would be like rebelling against the Crown. He and his seventy rebels retired to Xaragua to see if they, too, could get the hospitality of Behechio's kingdom.

An accomplice of Roldán, the cacique Guarionex of the province called Magua, retreated to the mountains, where one of the fierce tribes gave him refuge. The tribe had opposed Columbus on the first voyage, and if they now admonished Guarionex and the rest of the caciques for bringing this trouble upon themselves and upon the whole of Haiti, they could hardly have been considered wrong. And now even more trouble was to befall them. For, not wishing to pursue Roldán at the court of the generous Behechio, Bartholomew Columbus and his men turned upon Guarionex, burning villages in their punitive expedition, capturing Guarionex and his host and subduing that part of the island.

This was what Christopher Columbus met when he sailed into the new settlement of Santo Domingo. As ruthless as he himself had been, the natives of the island had seen even greater ruthlessness, and although they were 'pacified', which meant they were now helpless, they were restive. The rebellious Roldán was at large in Xaragua. About one third of his 500 men were ill with syphilis, and no doubt contaminating the whole of Xaragua with it. Even more serious perhaps was that the three caravels Columbus had sent directly to Haiti from the Canary Islands had over-run Santo Domingo and came to anchor at Xaragua, near Roldán's headquarters. Not knowing what had happened they had allowed Roldán to induce them ashore and there he managed to encourage a great number of them to rebel against the 'foreigner'. Many of those seamen were tough criminals from Spanish jails, and glad to do what they could do best – fight. Roldán raised a sizeable army and now decided on a trial of strength. On the other hand, Christopher Columbus, who was completely taken aback by those developments, could raise only seventy armed men to confront Roldán.

It was at this time that Columbus, realising that he needed more reinforcements in Santo Domingo, quickly despatched his own flagship as well as the *Correo*, to Spain, and kept the *Vaqueños*, which he appeared to like. It was not a case of desperation for he did not think that Roldán would attack, but he took note of the treachery of some of the men, and badly needed men he could count on. He felt that the most dangerous enemies of the Spaniards were the Spanish rebels themselves, who knew the use of arms and who could easily ambush, and also mobilise armies of natives as Roldán was doing. What he wanted to do was to capture as many as he could of the rebellious soldiers and send them back to Spain, meantime replacing them with new people whom he hoped the caravels would bring back from Spain. He had to wait patiently on the ships, for in any case he could do little with his seventy men. He also badly needed provisions of course.

With the two caravels now returning to Spain he sent his account of his new discoveries to the sovereigns. He told them about his encounter with an island he named Trinidad, thereby fulfilling his promise; he told them about the cacique of Paria, about the prospect of pearls, about the great freshwater sea – in fact it was this account that has given information of the voyage. One of the interesting things that comes out of the account is that Columbus, in dead earnest, believed that particular area of Trinidad and Paria was the 'Terrestrial Paradise' referred to in the Bible, and advanced several arguments why it was bound to be so. On another matter, perhaps hoping that the sovereigns would drop their objection to the enslavement of the natives, he said he was sending 'In the name of the Holy Trinity', all the slaves that could be sold, and brazil-wood', in order to contribute to the huge cost of establishing a colony. He also requested that devoted priests be sent out to help convert the 'Indians', because the only priest that had come out on the second voyage, Fray Ramon Pane, could not do it all by himself. He asked for clothing, and wine, saying that the island could now provide its own meat, and there was a lot of cassava bread. Describing the bad example that was being shown by Roldán, and the great threat that Roldán was posing to the peace of Española, he declared that men and ships were needed with great urgency to reduce Roldán to order.

Columbus was so intent on avoiding a confrontation with Roldán, perhaps to give the impression to the natives that the strangers were united, that he thought the best strategy was to 'sweeten' the rebel. Shortly after the caravels left he sent a note to Roldán saying he knew his dear friend wanted to go home but that he could detain the ships no longer because the slaves were dying. He offered a peace conference. The caravels had left in mid-October and by November an agreement was signed allowing Roldán's followers a free passage to Spain, with their gold, concubines, and slaves. Columbus promised to provide a ship within fifty days, but could not, and Roldán raised his terms. The new terms called on Columbus to restore Roldán to the office of Chief Justice, to declare that all charges made against him were false, and to make grants of land in the province of Xaragua for those who chose to remain. The admiral tried hard to avoid further humiliating himself and the Crown, but finally signed the

Fig.45 Indians working, a scene from Oviedo's *La hystoria generale de las Indias,* 1547

agreement in September 1499.

In fact, the granting of the land in this case started the system of *encomiendas*. Each of Roldán's settlers was allotted a large plot of cultivated land, upon which there was to be, as a start, 10,000 cassava plants. (Bear in mind that this had been the territory of the great Behechio, who, in mid-1496, had so sumptuously entertained Bartholomew Columbus. By 1499, due to the constant repression and injustice of the Spaniards, no cacique was master of any tract of land in Haiti. The Crown of Spain owned everything.) Christopher Columbus granted this land, along with the people that were on it, according to the contract, 'to have and to hold and to exploit as the grantee saw fit'. The caciques could not frown on this because it meant that those of them who had remained with their lives were now free of the burdensome tributes of gold.

Intrigues and Conspiracies

When, in October 1499, Columbus sent two more caravels back to Spain, he sent, by the same opportunity, letters to the sovereigns explaining the *encomienda* arrangement as well as other agreements he had come to with Roldán, declaring that they had been made under duress, and asking that a competent judge be sent out there to help him govern the island. It would only have been human if the sovereigns of Spain had eventually got fed up with Columbus.

But it is the voyage of the previous two caravels that is the point to consider. When the *Correo* and the admiral's flagship had arrived in Spain in October 1498 with news of Paria and the 'Terrestrial Paradise', Alonso de Hojeda managed to get hold of the admiral's chart and decided to make a voyage to that region. He sailed with the pilot Bartholomew Roldán, with the map-maker Juan de la Cosa, and with Amerigo Vespucci, all men who had coveted what the admiral had left behind in the 'Terrestrial Paradise', and who were bent on making the journey back.

Hojeda followed the precise path of Christopher Columbus, coming through what is now called the Columbus Channel, entering Kairi, or Trinidad, through the Serpent's Mouth and getting into 'the fresh-water sea' which is the Gulf of Paria. They apparently landed on Kairi, for Vespucci is recorded as having captured numerous people on this island. The explorers proceeded to Margarita for the express purpose of exploiting the pearl fisheries. Hojeda continued along the northern Paria coast to the westward, and apart from noting features of the coast, he found the islands now named Aruba, Bonaire, and Curacao. Two other noteworthy names arose from that expedition. Firstly, while Hojeda was exploring the northern shore of the continent, just south of Aruba he entered a little channel to find a huge lake, a lake that the natives of the place called 'Maracaibo'. In the lake itself there were many dwellings on stilts, and it surely must have been Vespucci, the Italian from Florence, who remarked that the scene reminded him of Venice, the famous Italian city built on water. The Italian name for Venice is Venezia, and so the place was named 'Venezuela', which has become the name of the whole country.

The other name of note again involves Amerigo Vespucci. In respect of that voyage Vespucci later wrote a letter to a friend in which he claimed to have reached the mainland of the 'New World' in 1497. Amerigo's untrue account was published in Lorraine, France, in 1507, and, as a tribute to Amerigo a chart of the continent carried the name 'America'.

Hojeda and his men at length continued the voyage to Haiti, and when Christopher Columbus heard that Hojeda had been on a voyage of discovery Columbus tried to have him and his men arrested. But Hojeda got away, scudded to the archipelago of small islands north of Haiti and Cuba, captured a great number of people as slaves, and set sail for Spain.

Judgement for the Brothers Columbus

There was no doubt at all that the three Columbus brothers, Bartholomew, Diego, and Christopher had performed poorly in trying to administer the settlements in Haiti – firstly Ysabella, and when Ysabella was abandoned, Santo Domingo. They had given considerable help to their enemies in creating a loss of confidence in their administration, and if Queen Isabella, on receiving the Roldán letter of October 1498, had thrown up her hands to heaven in despair, she had to be commended for not having lost her patience until now. For the agreement reached with Roldán was scandalous. How could Columbus let Francisco Roldán usurp his authority – which, after all, was *her* authority? Then, too, he was hypocritically asking for priests to convert the native peoples to Christianity, something she was always advocating, but was he not at the same time constantly flouting her authority by sending boatloads of 'Indians' to Spain to be sold in the slave markets? Another thing he asked for was an educated and experienced man to administer justice. That was exactly what was needed. She would send out a man who would be completely free to do what he wanted, would take orders from no one, would observe exactly what was happening and would dispense justice without fear or favour. She had sided with Christopher Columbus for too long. Now she was washing her hands of bias.

In early 1499 the sovereigns of Spain selected Francisco de Bobadilla to go out to Haiti as Chief Justice and to conduct an enquiry into the affairs of Santo Domingo. Bobadilla had a high reputation as an upright and honest man. He had served at the court many years before, and among honours that had come to him was the equivalent of a knighthood. The sovereigns gave him full powers for his assignment in Haiti. He had powers to arrest anyone, and he was also requested to take over all forts and other royal property from the admiral, who was commanded to obey his orders.

When Bobadilla entered the harbour of Santo Domingo what he saw must have made up his mind for him on a matter which was hard to believe. He must have had difficulty in believing the many stories of cruelty he had heard about Columbus by detractors and enemies, for the Columbus he had seen in Spain was always in monk's dress, was always praying, was always gentle. But what could greet his eyes as he entered the harbour? The corpses of seven Spaniards were hanging from a gallows! When he landed, Diego Columbus, who was in charge of the city, (and probably did not know who Bobadilla was) told him that five more people were due to hang next day. A furious Bobadilla ordered Diego to hand over the

Fig.46   Columbus being taken prisoner by Bobadilla on Española, from *Americae Partes* published 1590, de Bry 1613

prisoners. Diego refused. Bobadilla read his commissions, called on the people to obey his orders in the name of the king and queen of Spain, and took over the citadel, and also took over the admiral's house, and impounded his papers and other effects. Then he clamped Diego Columbus in irons, and when Christopher Columbus, who was absent from the city, returned, he threw him into jail. Bartholomew, who was at large with an armed force, was prevailed upon by his brothers to submit peacefully, and he was also put in irons aboard a ship. Bobadilla, who then took evidence relating to the charges against the Columbus brothers, and deliberated on this, ruled, rather leniently, that they be sent to Spain for trial.

In October 1500 the brothers Diego and Christopher Columbus left Santo Domingo in chains for trial in Spain. No sooner had they left the harbour than the captain offered to remove the admiral's chains, but the admiral replied: 'Let them stay. They have been put there in the sovereigns' name, and I will wear them until the sovereigns order them to be removed.'

And thus the third voyage ended with pain for Christopher Columbus. He would remain in Spain for some time and mope and grieve, but, amazingly, he would return to favour again, and he would cross the western seas yet another time.

CHAPTER FIVE
The Fourth Voyage

On 9th May 1502, Christopher Columbus set out on his final voyage of discovery. Between the time that he had been sent back to Spain in chains, 1498, and this moment, he seems to have aged considerably. Certainly he had worried a lot. He had worried about little things and about big things, and in some matters his views were perfectly justified, while in others they seemed to be bordering on pettiness.

Columbus was deeply hurt about having been sent back to Spain in chains. He was very much aware of the great contribution he had made to exploration and he found it scandalous that people should try to humiliate him, to disrespect him and on the whole to act as if he did not matter. Also he could not understand how it was that the sovereigns of Spain could have been so busy that he had had to remain in chains for about six weeks after his arrival in Spain before they ordered him to be released and summoned him before them to hear his story. After all, had he not given them an entire 'New World'? It was of little importance to him to hear that matters of state took up their time, that there was the secret Treaty of Granada seizing the attention of Ferdinand the Catholic and Louis XII of France, both poised to share the Kingdom of Naples.

Columbus was also peeved that Hojeda and Vespucci had been allowed to sail from Spain in 1499, to search for wealth – particularly the pearl fisheries of Margarita – and to make new discoveries, for he saw this as his preserve and his alone. It was only human for Columbus to feel that all must fall in behind the 'Admiral of the Ocean Sea', who was the first to show the way, and one whose deeds none could equal.

Regarding the first-cited grievance, if Columbus could not forgive Ferdinand and Isabella for not rushing to his side and casting off his shackles, perhaps he could forgive them even less for the withdrawal of his rights and privileges in Haiti by Francisco de Bobadilla. What he really wanted to see was Bobadilla recalled to Spain and punished and the king and queen apologising for what had happened and declaring that all his rights were intact, just as before.

But the king and queen had done no such thing. Yet they knew how to be gracious to Columbus, and it appears that the admiral craved their every kind word, their every smile. Although in the view of the sovereigns Columbus was hopeless as an administrator, and apart from that, had done many cruel things against their wishes, they could never bring themselves to be severe and off-hand with him. Thus, despite all the adversities and problems, when, in 1502, he approached them for a fourth expedition to the 'Indias', they found it impossible to turn away from him.

They provided a fleet of four caravels: *La Capitana*, which was the flagship; *Santiago de Palos*, which had Bartholomew Columbus aboard, *La Gallega*, captained by Pedro de Terreros, and *Vizcaiña*, which was the smallest of the caravels, captained by a young Genoese, Bartolomeo Fieschi.

The admiral, who had his fourteen-year-old son, Ferdinand, with him, sailed from Cadiz but had barely got out to sea when a strong south-westerly wind forced him to seek shelter. For two days they awaited a change of wind and on 11th May they struck out into open sea.

Ferdinand Columbus was probably not the youngest aboard on this voyage. There were fifty-six youths aboard, some of them being as young as twelve and thirteen. According to Ferdinand the complete personnel in the four ships numbered 140, which meant that young boys made up forty per cent of the crew. Why was this voyage so full of children? Was it an attempt to avoid the constant friction in respect to the women, or was it simply a question of not having enough money to pay men?

With his sails full of wind, on 20th May the admiral reached the Canary Islands, and he tarried there a little while, taking on wood and water at Grand Canary. On the 25th he left Ferro, his favourite jumping-off point, and he was now on his path

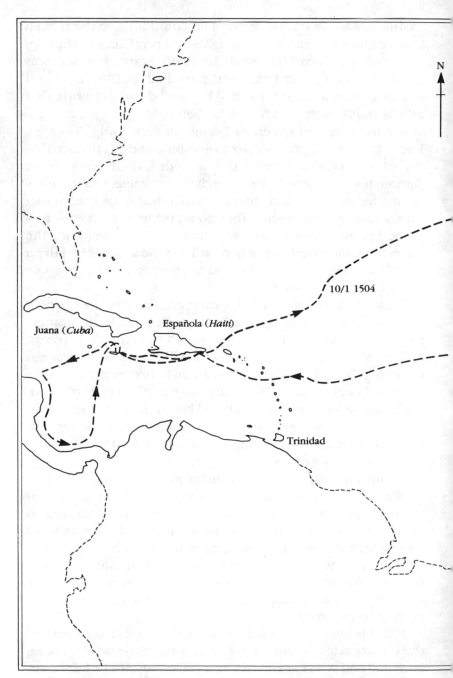

Fig.47   The course of Columbus' fourth voyage

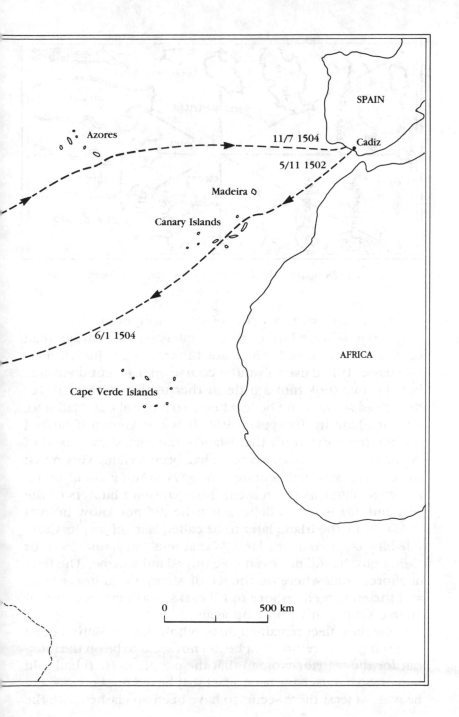

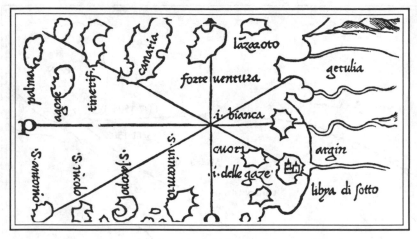

Fig.48   A 1528 map of the Canary Islands from Bordone's *Isolario*

to the 'Indias', with his course set west-by-south.

The winds were kinder to Columbus on this voyage than on any of the others, for he made the crossing in just twenty-one days. He had used a similar course on his second voyage, but this one took him a little further to the southward, for he arrived at the island he had heard so much about, Matinino, on 15th June in that year 1502. It is not known if he had deliberately steered for that island – the legendary 'Island of Women' – for it was an island he had been wishing very much to see. Yet, strangely enough, he says nothing about them, not even about its Carib men, those constant hunters of the sea, and one is led to believe that he did not know he was in Matinino, the island later to be called Martinique. Its Carib inhabitants called their island 'Wanacaera'. Most untypical for Columbus, he did not even give this island a name. The fleet anchored somewhere on the lee of Matinino, in heavy seas, and the crew went ashore to fill casks, wash clothes, and of course simply to be on land again.

Columbus' fleet remained three whole days in Matinino, all the stranger, therefore, that he did not seem to be on the look-out for the warrior-women that the people in Haiti had told him of. So it must have been a fact that he did not know where he was. At least there seems to have been no clashes with the natives. The white tribe may have taken aboard a great deal of cassava bread and yams, which seemed so delicious to them on earlier voyages. At least Columbus was charmed with the place, for in his usual style of exaggeration he called it 'the prettiest, most fertile, and mildest country in the world'.

While in Matinino itself, or in those waters, Columbus and his men were bound to see that nearby island to the south. Although Ferdinand mentions it, neither he nor his father speaks of the name. The island is what we know today as St Lucia. A popular account says that he encountered it on St Lucy's Day in 1502, and called it Santa Lucia after the saint. But Columbus was in those waters from about the 14th of June to the 19th of June 1502 and St Lucy's Day is on the 13th of December. It seems clear, therefore, that it was later Spaniards who named it – or rather, renamed it, for this was the lush Hewanorra of the Caribs. Almost the same story must be told of another island slightly to the south-west of St Lucia and distant by a few leagues. There is no doubt at all that the Spaniards saw the high mountains of this island which we know today as St Vincent. The Caribs called their island Hairoun, which means 'Home of the Blessed', and it might have been a blessed omen that the Spaniards did not get to it. Popular histories in respect of St Vincent say that Christopher Columbus encountered it on St Vincent's Day in 1498. However, St Vincent's Day is on the 22nd January, and on the 22nd of January 1498 Columbus was in Spain. It was not until 31st May in that year 1498 that he was to leave Spain on his third voyage.

However, the year one is looking at is 1502, and the Spaniards, having stayed three days in Matinino, resumed their voyage on 18th June, turning north to the island Columbus had called 'Dominica'. It appears that the fierce Caribs again fought him off from the shores of Wy-tou-Koubouli, their island home, as they had fought him off in 1493. The admiral, who could not have been very interested in landing, then went along the chain of islands which he had already encountered on his second voyage, and on 29th June he reached Haiti, stealing into the waters of the settlement of Santo Domingo.

And 'stealing' is not too harsh a word, for the Spanish

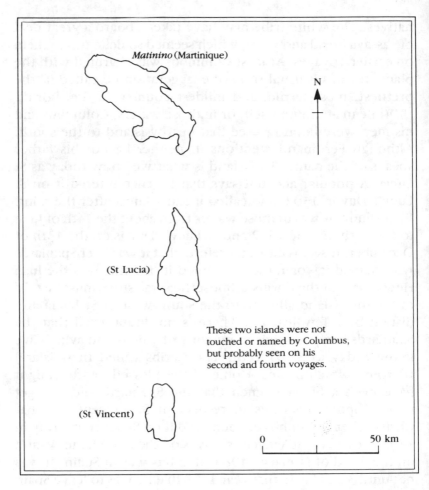

Matinino (Martinique)

N

(St Lucia)

These two islands were not
touched or named by Columbus,
but probably seen on his
second and fourth voyages.

(St Vincent)

0   50 km

Fig.49   Martinique, St Lucia and St Vincent

sovereigns had expressly forbidden him to visit Santo
Domingo. For they knew well how bitter and angry he was
with the officials there. The fact that he had been sent back
from Haiti in chains was only one of the issues he was still
riled about. Columbus looked upon all the royal officials there
as imposters, and deeply felt that he alone and his brothers
were entitled to give orders in Haiti. 'It is I who dared the
sea of darkness', he seemed to tell everybody. 'It is I who
discovered this new world. Now they can come and strut
about!'

He truly took the attitude that he had 'discovered' these lands, not giving credit to the fact that he had met people there confirmed in their way of life and people who might have justly claimed that they discovered him.

Be that as it may, he sailed directly to Haiti and was now calling at Santo Domingo contrary to the wishes of the sovereigns of Spain.

And then something strange happened to show that the fates were always with Columbus. The newly-appointed Governor of Haiti, Don Nicolas de Ovando, had arrived three months before with a large fleet of thirty vessels. When Columbus arrived off Santo Domingo the fleet of Don Nicolas was about to leave for Spain. Columbus sent the *Gallega* ashore requesting permission for his fleet to enter, and advising that there was a storm ahead and that the homeward bound fleet should ride out the storm in port because it was dangerous to leave now.

The Governor, angry even to hear Columbus' name, was extremely scornful of the message. Firstly, he refused the admiral's request to come into port; then, reading the letter aloud to his men he joined them in making fun of Columbus' storm warning, calling the admiral a 'soothsayer', and Ovando directed the homeward-bound fleet to sail right away.

The large, fine-looking fleet had hardly cleared the island when the storm broke with all its fury. It ravaged the ships, driving some of them to the shore where they foundered against reefs and rocks. Nineteen ships went down with all aboard, and among those was the flagship itself, commanded by Columbus' friend, Antonio de Torres, and with him aboard, the admiral's bitter enemy, Francisco de Bobadilla. On that ship also was Guarionex, the conquered cacique; gold worth a considerable sum, as well as the largest nugget of gold the Spaniards had yet found in these 'Indias'. In that disaster over 500 lives were lost. Taking the news to Spain was the only vessel to reach there from that large fleet, the *Aguja*. This vessel, not highly thought of, was taking to Spain 4,000 pesos of Bobadilla's gold, and this gold was eventually received by Columbus' son, Don Diego Colón. It seemed as if the fates had performed witchcraft on Columbus' behalf.

When the storm had broken, Columbus, having been refused

entry into the harbour at Santo Domingo, took his fleet some
distance to the westward and anchored as close to the land
as possible. The storm maintained its speed but Columbus
had his ships well sheltered. That was on the 29th June. The
next day the ships left their anchorage and skidded before the
wind. All was 'plain sailing', but by nightfall the wind rose
again. It was a most horrible night, with the wind howling
fiercely and assaulting the ships, which tried to anchor. The
Capitana's anchor remained firm, but the other ships were
torn from their anchoring place. It was pitch-black, and as the
ships' crews battled the hurricane no ship's company knew
whether the other ships were lost or not. Columbus wrote
in his log: 'What man born, not excepting Job, would not have
died of despair, when in such weather, seeking safety for my
son, my brother, my shipmates and myself, we were forbidden
the land and the harbours that I, by God's will and sweating
blood, had won for Spain?'

The *Santiago* was all but lost in that storm, but Bartholomew
Columbus, who as well as Ferdinand, fought hard to save
her, succeeded against all the odds. Slightly younger than
Christopher, Bartholomew amply justified Ferdinand's
description of him as the best seaman of that fleet. On Sunday
3rd July the four vessels, *Capitana, Gallega, Santiago*, and
Vizcaíña emerged victorious from the 'Battle of the Hurricane'
and met in rendezvous in a land-locked harbour, which they
named 'Puerto Escondido', (Hidden Port).

From that harbour the gallant little fleet rounded Beata
Island near Cape Beata, the southernmost point of Haiti, and
then ran into an inlet which Columbus called Puerto Brazil,
a place later to become Jacmel, seeking this harbour to avoid
another threatening storm. No storm came, however, and the
fleet left, never to visit Haiti again.

When Columbus had left Spain on the fourth voyage to the
'Indias', his intention had been to follow the coast from
Margarita, in fact taking up where he had left off in 1498. This
was because the Paria cacique had told him it was the continent
and it was mainly to verify this and explore this continent that
he wanted to get back there. But at this stage sailing south
against the currents and in this season of treacherous storms

was quite out of the question. Already being so far north he decided to push out to the west, and see if he would encounter land, or if perhaps, there was a strait. As he pushed forward he came into a sudden and complete calm, and he drifted to some tiny coral islands. Columbus stayed just long enough there for his men to get water by sinking wells in the sand and, consequently, for him to name the island 'La Isla de las Pozas' (Island of the Wells). When he left, intending to continue west, a north-westerly current took the fleet north of Jamaica, between islands later called the Caymans. Between 24th and 27th July he remained anchored off one of those little islands and on that day, 27th July he was able to do a good run. He completed nearly 400 miles in three days. At that point they saw what they thought to be an island in the distance. It was Bonacca, one of the islands off the coast of Honduras.

Columbus seemed to know very well that ahead lay the mainland or terra firma, and that this was a continuation of the land from the coast of Paria and of the coastline that ran west from just south of Margarita. How did he know this? Neither Columbus nor the majority of historians who have written of his voyages have made a point of mentioning this, but it is clear that much of what has passed for the admiral's intuition and skill was information given to him by his native guides.

Columbus himself has not helped in enabling us to see things in their true light. For example, when he reached so far westerly that he was in the vicinity of the mainland, he wrote: 'No one had sailed as far as this region.' What then, about the native seamen? Did they not exist? The islanders in their canoes had covered the entire region, as Columbus found out, and he had the good fortune to benefit constantly from their knowledge – not only their geographical knowledge, but their knowledge of tropical weather conditions in general, and in particular of signs of storms.

Columbus was very much impressed when he arrived at Bonacca Island, for the native canoes he saw there gave him a high opinion of the advancement of the sea-going men of those parts, and more than ever, the merchandise with which they were trading. The merchandise he saw was so rich that

for the first time he had glimpses of that world reflected by
Marco Polo. None could have blamed him for believing that
he was finally in the precincts of Cathay, and near to the
doorstep of the Great Khan. In fact, he had the experience
both of the sea-going craft and the merchandise, at the same
moment. No sooner had his fleet cast anchor at Bonacca Island
than a canoe as long as a galley-ship and several feet broad,
pulled up alongside the *Capitana*. (They were no doubt called
to the flagship by the native guides.) The canoe had a crew
of twenty-five men with a great number of women and
children as passengers, and these passengers were sheltered
by a waterproof awning. Obviously the canoe was trading as
a ferry. She was going about her own business when the
Spaniards arrived, and true to their method, the Spaniards
captured her, plundered her merchandise, and seized some
of her crew. On inspection of the merchandise the Spaniards

Fig.50   Cocao pods drying and on the tree, from Benzoni's
Historia del Mondo Nuovo, 1563

found there were cotton (cloth) coverings and shawls; vests, colourfully dyed; woven material, fineries as shawls of such designs which put the Spaniards in mind of the dress of the Moorish women in Spain; wooden swords with edges of flint, copper hatchets as well as bells; crucibles for the melting of copper. The foodstuff consisted of roots and grains that the Spaniards had already seen, but what they had not come across was a liquor that Columbus found tasted like English beer. Also, what the strangers had not found before was any notion of currency such as they used here. This was a bean, apparently beans from the tree that the Spaniards were to get to know as *cacao*. Concerning the people on the boat, Columbus was so struck by the women modestly covering their faces that he ordered his men to leave them well alone – which, of course, was an ineffective command.

Columbus was now searching for a strait, for in his mind it was beyond this strait that lay the riches and splendours he had come so far to find. He had come to this conclusion after studying his three previous voyages, the folklore and fantasies then current, and more than ever the stories he had heard from the native rovers of these seas. Or was it simply his interpretation of these stories? Was he stubbornly believing that there just had to be a strait?

From Bonacca, Columbus made for the mainland, which was not more than 30 miles away. They arrived at a point on the mainland which, according to Ferdinand Columbus, the admiral called 'Punta Caxinas' from the name of a kind of tree that was plentiful there. The area today is known as Cape Honduras.

Sunday 14th August was a big day for Columbus for this was the day that he took formal possession of the mainland of this 'New World' for the king and queen of Spain. Again the question is asked: what would the natives have thought could they have followed what was going on? Hundreds of them came to see the 'taking-of-possession ceremony'. Could they have believed it was possible that members of this strange tribe, whom they had befriended, could actually be taking possession of their land for a distant cacique? The inhabitants who came down to witness the ceremony made a veritable

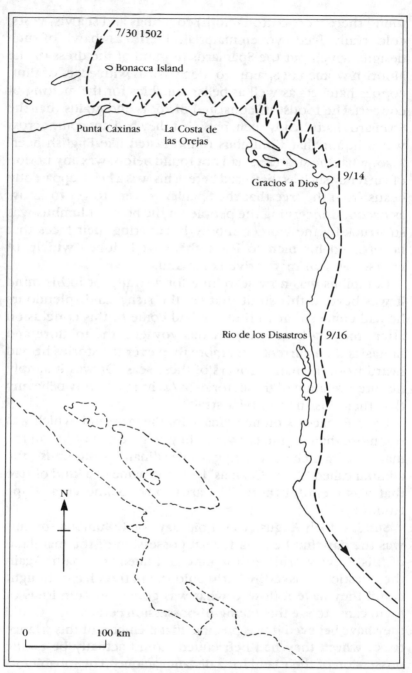

Fig. 51   Bonacco Island, la Costa de las Orejas and the journey south

bazaar of the occasion, bringing, among other things, 'fowls of the country, which are better than ours, roast fish, and red and white beans', according to Columbus. Assuming that in this case Columbus' information is reliable, then the 'fowls of the country, which are better than ours', were probably turkeys, birds which are native to that area, and which Hernan Cortez and his men nearly two decades later, have been said to be the first Spaniards to see. Columbus spoke of the inhabitants as 'mostly naked, their bodies tattoooed or painted with designs like lions, deer, and turretted castles'. Surely we must be used to Columbus by now not to place much importance on these last words, for there being no lions in that part of the world, and certainly no turretted castles at that time, it is not possible that the admiral could have seen that. But as usual among the fantasy in Columbus' statements, are several glimmers of fact – at least, things that seem credible. For example he said he saw some of the inhabitants with their faces painted red and black, and ears bored so as to leave large gaping holes. Such people were known to have inhabited that coast. In fact, he named the coast 'La Costa de las Orejas' or 'The Coast of the Ears'.

Columbus described the 'newly-discovered' land as 'verdant and beautiful, low, with pines, oaks, and palms, and an abundance of wildlife like pumas, deer, and gazelles'. (This was another of the inaccuracies of Christopher Columbus. He could not have seen gazelles in those parts.)

Columbus' joy of having at last got to the mainland – something he was sure of now – was greatly tempered by the ruthless weather he was encountering day by day. The taking-of-possession ceremony seems to have been at a harbour where the Spaniards later founded a city called Trujillo, and Columbus was attempting to follow the coastline which ran east then curved south, then swept east again. (He did not know this yet, of course, for he had in mind getting back to where he had left off, at Margarita, on the third voyage.) He did not get very far. Fighting to sail down the coast, the fleet was bludgeoned by head winds and violent weather continuously for twenty-eight days, anchoring every night as close as possible to the land. It was the hurricane season, of course, but Columbus could not understand it, and he must have joined the crew, who, frightened, fell on their knees and asked God's forgiveness for all the wrongs they had done. He declared: 'It was one continual rain, thunder and lightning. The ships lay with sails torn, and anchors, rigging, cables, boats, and many of the stores lost. The crew were making vows to be good, to go on pilgrimages, etc., even hearing one another's confessions. Other tempests I have seen but none that lasted so long as this, nor so grim . . . What gripped me most was the sufferings of my son. To think that so young a lad, only 13, should go through so much. But the Lord gave him such courage that he heartened the rest, and worked as hard as if he had been at sea all his life. I was sick and many times lay at death's door, and gave orders from a dog-house that the people clapped together for me from the poop deck. My brother was in the worst of the ships and I felt terribly for having pursuaded him to come on the voyage against his will.'

However, at that point, the worst was over. There was no strait in sight, but the next day, 14th September, the fleet came to a cape, beyond which the coast dipped and ran due south, and the wind actually died away, and there were favourable currents. Columbus and his Spaniards could hardly believe their good fortune. The admiral, relieved, named this headland, 'Cape Gracias a Dios' – in English, 'Cape Thanks be to God'.

Columbus rode down the southern shore, presumably still on the look-out for the strait to Cathay, but apart from the fact that there was no strait, nothing unexpected happened until 16th September when he came to the mouth of a wide and pleasant-looking river, in front of which he anchored. He sent the ships' boats to shore to collect wood and to get some water from the river. While there, the wind rose and whipped up angry waves which swamped the boats. Two seamen lost their lives. Columbus named the river 'Rio do los Disastros' (River of the Disasters). The river of the disasters was quite likely what became known as the Rio Grande.

They continued down the southward running coast for several days, keeping a sharp look-out, and apparently sailing in the day and anchoring in the night for fear of islets and

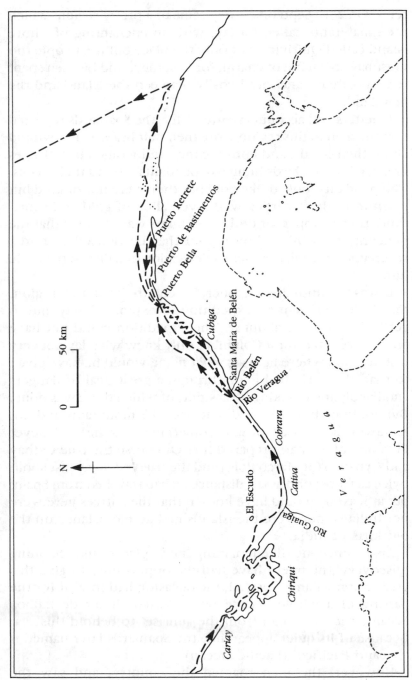

Fig.52 Columbus' exploration of Veragua and what we now call Panama

reefs. On 25th September they came to a pretty region, which the inhabitants called Cariay, with an enchanting off-shore island called Quiriviri. Not only the place but the people too must have been full of charm, for Columbus and his men spent ten days there, anchored cosily between the island and the mainland.

In letters and accounts written later, the Spaniards reported that the men in this region wore their hair braided and wound about their heads, and both the men and women had effigies of eagle-looking birds hung like pendants around their necks. The pendants looked like gold but they were not of gold but *guanin*, in these parts a well-loved alloy of gold and sometimes tin or copper, or both. Columbus was so upset that the pendants were not of pure gold that he refused to trade, whereupon the villagers sent a delegation of ladies to persuade him.

It was not until 2nd October, his eighth day in that region, that Columbus sent an expedition to explore Cariay and to get to know more about it. The expedition could not have reached very far, for if Columbus only knew what lay not very distant from where he was, what name would he have given to that place? He had gone through a great deal of dangers and tribulations looking for a strait, of which there was none. But could he have guessed that over the mountains and not far away lay a vast ocean, something that he had never dreamed of, or had prepared for? Of course the true Cathay and Cypango (of Marco Polo) and the true India, lay just about twice as far beyond as the distance he had travelled from Spain, but at least he would have known that the natives here were not Indians, nor were the islands he had met islands on the outskirts of India.

Also, since he liked naming new places and claiming 'discovery', he might have had the opportunity to give this great water a name. Instead, the occasion had to wait for the passing of a whole decade when Vasco Nuñez de Balboa became the first 'man from the sunrise' to behold this sea. Because of its quiet appearance the Spaniards later named it 'Oceano Pacifico' (Pacific Ocean).

However, the men roamed the country, and saw the

landscape to advantage, and they were particularly impressed with the abundance and variety of wild animals, as compared to the sparseness of these creatures in the islands they had previously explored. They reported seeing a lot of deer and pumas, and Columbus himself spoke of a 'very great fowl, with feathers like wool'. No such fowl is known but it may have been one of the species of turkey.

One of the things they saw that has stirred historians was an impressive wooden structure covered with reeds, and within which structure was a number of burial places. In one of the tombs was a tablet on which was carved the likeness of the dead person – but not the name, for apparently these clever people did not develop the art of writing. The corpse, which lay head downwards, was adorned with beads and ornaments of *guanin*.

Columbus said he was told that there were great copper mines in the country, and that from the copper they made hatchets and other elaborate articles, both cast and soldered. They also made forges, some with crucibles, and other conveniences for the goldsmith.

These must certainly have been a different, more highly advanced people than the rest they had met, for Columbus declared, 'Here they go clothed. And in that province I saw some very large sheets of cotton cloth, very elaborately and cleverly worked, and others very delicately pencilled in colours. They tell me that more inland, towards Cathay, they have cloths interwoven with gold.' Towards Cathay indeed!

Columbus said that for want of an interpreter they were able to learn very little of the country or what it contained. For although the country was thickly populated, he explained, each 'nation' had a different language. The admiral said, 'Indeed, so much so that they can no more understand each other than we can understand the Arabs.'

Columbus and his men finally left Cariay on Wednesday 5th October and sailed along the coastline, turning in a south-easterly direction. Columbus, looking for the non-existent strait, was misled again when he saw what looked like a channel in the land, but it only led to a bay. Curious it is that about four centuries later, a 'strait' – the Panama Canal – was cut in just that area.

This was a strange part of the voyage in that Columbus appears to have ceased to look for a strait from here on, for he mentions nothing of it, yet we are sure that he never even attempted to find the 'Great Water' on the other side of the land, although now he was told that he was sailing beside a narrow isthmus. It is even stranger to realise that the fleet, sailing further down the coast, spent three months in Veragua, around the narrowest part of the isthmus, and constantly in touch with the natives, without Columbus once alluding to isthmus in his letters, let alone appearing to know that he had the key to the 'Great Water'.

Anyway, according to the admiral's letters, when he had reached Chiriqui, he had heard that he was in a land of gold, and from the information he received from the inhabitants at Chiriqui, as well as from his own interpreters, he gave the impression that a nearby province called Ciguare was really the Ciamba (Cochin-China) of Marco Polo. If he felt this way, perhaps there was no need to continue looking for a strait.

It may have been a conspiracy between the native inter-preters and the inhabitants of Chiriqui and the country around, that Columbus and his crew heard many tall tales of Ciguare, and of unlimited gold and precious stones. Columbus himself, in order to ascertain if he was really in the Orient mentioned to his guides certain names that Ptolemy had mentioned and sights that Marco Polo had beheld. They told him yes, this was the place. And even more so than on the first voyage, he was now sure gold was at hand, because he saw abundant golden ornaments about.

Letters from Columbus at about this time inform the sover-eigns of Spain that he was near to the 'Golden Chersonese' that Ptolemy had written of. He talks of the Ciambans (Ciguareans) as great traders, and says the River Ganges was but ten days sail from their shores. He told the sovereigns that they were not naked savages, these Ciambans, but went about armed with swords, and that they used cavalry in battle, and that they had warships equipped with cannons. Judging from the fact that the inhabitants of those provinces had experience neither of rich garments, nor cavalry, nor cannons, nor warships, it is either that Columbus asked questions about these things and got the expected answers, or that he was deliberately misleading Ferdinand and Isabella – and not for the first time.

It is more likely though that the 'Admiral of the Ocean Sea' asked questions and believed the answers he got, for otherwise he would hardly have remained three long months in this region, even making allowances for the bad weather.

After leaving Chiriqui, on 17th October, the admiral went out to sea, passing near an island he named 'El Escudo', maybe through its resemblance to an *escudo* or shield. Then they ran southward about 38 miles and anchored at the mouth of a river the people called Guaiga, and in a region called Veragua. (It must be taken into account that the Spaniards, without intentionally doing so, made every word they heard Spanish-sounding, and maybe not one of the native words sounded exactly as the Spaniards rendered it. 'Veragua' seems to be a case in point.) Veragua, the inhabitants told Columbus, was an important source of gold.

On this coast, described by later explorers as 'inhospitable', Columbus obtained a certain amount of discs of pure gold, but he also experienced a great deal of harrassment. Or maybe it should be said that it was the inhabitants of this region who were harrassed, since the visitors had disturbed them in their home. When the Spanish fleet had anchored off the River Guaiga the great desire of the crew was to make contact with the inhabitants for the purpose, clearly, of obtaining gold. They saw some of the inhabitants on 20th October, but these were hostile and there were several skirmishes. However, between these interludes came moments of peace, when they were able to trade worthless trifles for discs of pure gold.

Despite the fact that this part of the coast was without harbours, and that the narrow coastal plain was soon superseded by high, craggy, terrain, and jungle forests, Columbus delayed here greatly because he wanted to see the source of the gold ornaments being worn by the inhabitants, and he was most anxious to find the gold mines that some of his guides assured him were nearby. The Spaniards all appeared to be consumed by the thoughts of the amount of gold they were likely to find in this region, and later Columbus was to declare to the sovereigns of Spain: 'I saw more signs of gold in Veragua in two days than I saw in Española in four years.' Indeed, they were so excited that apparently no one wrote any letters, or put down his thoughts, which would have assisted greatly in finding out more about the area at that time, and what took place on this part of the voyage. Ferdinand Columbus alone describes what happened, and this was years later. At the time his father was exploring Veragua Ferdinand was fourteen years old and was taking part in everything. So he knew what was happening and appears to have had a lively memory. But he gives few dates, and therefore has not been of much help to historians.

Sailing down the coast from Guaiga, the Spaniards came to a place called Cativa, and Ferdinand writes: 'This was the first place in the Indias where we saw signs of a building. It was a great mass of stucco which appears to have been built of stone and lime. The admiral ordered a piece to be taken as a souvenir of that old building.' Was Cativa the site of an old civilisation?

With the coast running eastwardly, after Cativa came a province called Cobraba, which the admiral did not stop to investigate, since the coastline had no harbours. According to Ferdinand, after Cobraba, the fleet came to five villages of great trade, one of which was Veragua, where, he said, the gold was collected. Then they came to the village of Cubiga, at which place some guides that the Spaniards had kidnapped at Cariay told him they had come to the end of the 'trading country'.

It was at this point, with the admiral ready to turn back to go and investigate Veragua properly, and at least to find out from where the people were collecting the gold, that there came drama in the form of the weather. A particularly virulent rainy season had set in, with raging boisterous winds, especially the northerlies and westerlies. On the occasion when Columbus left Cubiga he wrote: 'There arose so violent a storm that we were forced to go wherever it drove us. I ran before the wind wherever it took me, without power to resist.' Certainly it is an ill wind that blows no good. When Columbus least expected it he found the fleet pushed into an excellent harbour. Columbus went on to describe the place: 'The country surrounding this harbour is not very rough but cultivated, and full of houses only a stone's throw or crossbow shot apart, pretty as a picture, the fairest things you ever saw. During the seven days that we tarried there on account of the rain and foul weather, canoes came constantly from the country around to barter all sorts of good things to eat and skeins of fine spun cotton, which they gave for trifles of brass such as lace points and tags.'

So it was very pleasant. Columbus was so pleased with this harbour that he named it 'Puerto Bello' or 'Lovely Port'. The date was Wednesday 2nd November 1502.

One week later, on Wednesday 9th November, Columbus left Puerto Bello and rounded a point which we know today as Manzanillo, and was following the coast further but the next day the wind rose up against the ships, forcing them back. Ferdinand, remembering the incident, said that they sheltered among islets, which turned out to be so full of maize that the admiral called the place 'Puerto de Bastimientos' or 'Harbour of Provisions'. (In 1508 it was re-named Nombre de Dios.) The fleet remained in this harbour a further twelve days, carrying out general repairs. When they left this port on Wednesday, 23rd November, the violent winds were still waiting for them, and it drove them back. Columbus said, 'But in again making for the port which I had quitted, I found on the way another port, which I named Retrete, where I put in for shelter with great peril and regret, and very weary, both I and the ships and my people.'

However, as weary as the sailors may have been, they never lost an opportunity for barter and trade, and indeed 'barter' and 'trade' were terms much too honourable for their dishonest approach, which was to wheedle as much gold and as many valuable objects as possible from the inhabitants in exchange for glass beads and hawks' bells. They remained in El Puerto del Retrete for a few days and this inlet was so narrow that the caravels had to lie almost alongside the bank. Fortunately the depth of water was good. The position of the caravels gave the men a fine opportunity for private trading,

and at night the most daring of them would slip away and take
the trail to the villages. Ferdinand Columbus, in speaking of
the crew sheltering from the storm at El Retrete mentioned

Fig.53   The Spaniards traded with the Indians wherever they could.
(From the Columbus letter, 1493)

the clandestine journeys to the villages. Many of these escapades did not remain secret, however, for as Ferdinand said, the men 'committed a thousand outrages, whence the Indians were provoked to alter their manners, and to break the peace, and some fights occurred between them.' In the end, large numbers of the inhabitants gathered threateningly near the ships, at which point, Columbus, failing to appease them with words, fired a cannon and scattered them.

Ferdinand apparently saw alligators at El Retrete, although one is by no means sure. He writes: 'In the harbour were vast lizards or crocodiles, which go out to sleep ashore . . . they are so ravenous and cruel that if they find a man asleep ashore they will drag him into the water to devour him . . .' This sounds like some of the stories of alligators. Since there is no report of a Spaniard being dragged into the water and devoured, what Ferdinand has related might be some of the tall stories told by the inhabitants to the Spaniards through their guides.

Since the high winds did not abate, Columbus, who had had his mind on returning to Veragua to find the gold mines, decided to go no further east along the coast, but to turn back. On Monday 5th December he left El Retrete, and that night he anchored at Puerto Bello. But the wicked winds did not intend to leave him alone. No sooner had he left port the next day, 6th December, than the winds swung round and battered the fleet, pushing them up and down between Puerto Bello and the Rio Chagres to the west. The admiral, who knew how to be melodramatic, but now not without cause, described the experience: 'The tempest arose and wearied me so that I knew not where to turn. My old wound opened up and for nine days I was lost, without hope of life. Eyes never beheld the sea so high, angry, and covered with foam. The wind not only prevented our progress, but offered no opportunity to run behind any headland for shelter . . . Never did the sky look more terrible; for one whole day and night it blazed like a furnace, and the lightning broke forth with such violence that each time I wondered if it had carried forth my spars and sails . . . All this time the water never ceased to fall from the sky. I do not say it rained, because it was like another deluge. The people were so worn out that they longed for death.'

This ordeal by the high winds lasted for a month. Fourteen-year-old Ferdinand bore witness to what he called 'the terrible storms', and he mentioned the occurrence on Tuesday 13th December of a water-spout which, he said, would have swamped the ships had they not dissolved it 'by reciting the Gospel according to St John'.

The ordeal continued. That same night the *Vizcaíña* lost sight of the other three, and only saw them again after three dark and frightening days. Then two days of calm followed but these brought more fear than relief. The caravels were surrounded by great schools of sharks. The only good side to this was that they feasted on shark meat, which was welcome, for their provisions were very low. Ferdinand touched on this point when he said, 'What with the heat and dampness, our ship's biscuit had become so wormy that, God help me, I saw many who waited for darkness to eat the porridge made of it, that they might not see the worms. Others were so used to eating them that they did not even trouble to pick them out, because they might lose their supper had they been so nice.'

Christmas was already in the air but it was not so much like Christmas for these 'strangers from the sunrise'. On Saturday 17th December they sneaked for shelter into an inlet called Huiva, which lay some 10 miles east of a rock they called Peñon. Here they rested three days. They reported that the inhabitants were tree-dwellers, although there does not seem to be any reason why this should be so. While they were in harbour the tempest was again waiting for them, and as soon as they emerged it blew up, enraged, and drove them into another harbour where they stayed for another three days. The admiral himself said of the wind: 'Like an enemy that lies in wait for a man, [the wind] assaulted us again, and forced us to Peñon, where, when we were hoping to enter the harbour, the wind, as if it were playing with us, started up so violently almost at the mouth of the harbour that it blew us back where we had been before.'

Columbus goes on: 'And here we stayed from the second day of the feast of the Nativity to the 3rd day of January 1503.' (The feast of the Nativity was on 26th December.) So the

Spaniards spent Christmas Day in the inlet called Huiva. Four hundred years later the Panama Canal was cut nearby.

One would think that with the buffeting that the ships took from the weather, and with the complaint of Columbus that he had been close to death from exhaustion, he would have taken the caravels *Capitana, Santiago, Vizcaiña*, and *Gallega* away as quickly as possible from that region. But not so. Columbus was bent on getting back to Veragua to find the mines of gold he was told about; and in general, the whole company wanted an opportunity to 'trade' and collect as much gold as they could.

So the four caravels took on a great deal of maize, as well as water, and firewood, and left what they called 'Puerto Gordo' on 3rd January 1503. It was not until 6th January that they reached a river 60 miles away, at the mouth of which Columbus anchored. This river he named 'Belén', which in English is Bethlehem, the birthplace of Christ. Here they did good business with the trifles they brought with them and of which they seemed to have had an unlimited supply.

The villages of the main inhabitants of the area, people known as the Guaymi, lay in the upper reaches of the River Belén and also the Veragua, which was close by. It was difficult to cross the sand-bars to get into the rivers but the thoughts of gold made the Spaniards extremely determined. With high tide, and choosing the right moment, each caravel took its chance and succeeded in getting over into the River Belén. There the river formed a comfortable basin, and all the four caravels seemed well accommodated. It was the rainy season, and the showers were pouring down ceaselessly. Columbus, in good heart, felt he would stay there until the rainy season was over.

On 12th January Bartholomew Columbus took the ships' boats and went up the River Veragua to the headquarters of a cacique the Spaniards were calling 'El Quibian'. Of course the Spaniards knew of him through their guides. El Quibian came downstream with a retinue of warriors to hold conference with the Spaniards, of whom he must have heard a great deal throughout many moons and rainy seasons. The encounter was pleasant and El Quibian gave the Spaniards permission to explore the rivers. The next day the cacique visited Columbus on the *Capitana*.

But rain was the great culprit in that bitter-sweet interlude. The Spaniards began their exploration immediately, but driving rains and floods and heavy seas breaking into the rivers prevented further exploration for a while. The high seas died down by early February and on the 6th Bartholomew Columbus, with three boats and sixty-eight men, went to the mouth of the Veragua River and rowed far upstream. Leaving the river in the interior they marched up-country with native guides and on the second day they found the coveted mines. In bushy, wooded country they found gold ore at their feet, and without any tools at all they collected a little gold and returned in safety. Only they knew of course that the Veragua of the stylish cacique, El Quibian, would never be the same again. They alone knew that the same cacique of whom they had asked permission to explore the rivers would now be swept aside, chased into the forest with his people, and would hardly have permission to live. In any case the land no longer belonged to El Quibian. Columbus had long since taken possession of it for the sovereign 'caciques' in Spain.

Christopher Columbus was elated to hear that his men had found the mines. He decided to build a town in Veragua and leave his brother Bartholomew in charge, while he went back to Spain to personally break the great news to the sovereigns and to get reinforcements and return.

At this point fortune favoured the Spaniards. The caciques and other villagers in the area showed warm friendship and did not even seem to be curious about the feverish exploration by the strangers and their keenness to get gold. Bartholomew with thirty Spaniards marched through villages yellow with the tassle of corn, or maize, but it was the yellow of gold that they were eager to see. These villagers also liked to wear gold pendants round their necks and the Spaniards obtained from them a great quantity of these ornaments, which they sent back to the ships.

Bartholomew Columbus returned and straightaway started work on the new settlement, called by his brother Christopher, 'Santa Maria de Belén'. The people appeared to allow the strangers to have their way, and it is highly likely that the

Fig.54 Indians making alcoholic drinks from maize, from Benzoni's
Historia del Mondo Nuovo, 1563

Spaniards had already instilled fear in them by firing a few
cannon shots. For these people, the Guaymis, seemed anything
but backward. They were skilled in handling gold, copper,
and tin, they were well advanced in the ways of fishing, they
were spinners and weavers of cotton into cloth, they had their
own cuisine based on cassava flour and maize, and they
brewed rather refined alcoholic drinks made from maize, as
well as from pineapples, which they cultivated for that
purpose. Although they had the odd custom of turning their
backs when they spoke, they were as a whole, clever and
observant. Yet they did not seem to observe at that time that
the welcome they were giving to Columbus was a welcome
to the quick end of their harmless but colourful days.

But even so, thanks to the despicable nature of so many of
the Spaniards, and thanks to the lack of any sort of respect

or consideration for their hosts, a change in the atmosphere of their relationship came at about this time. And as a matter of coincidence, what Columbus may well have been looking upon as the revenge of the native Gods continued to assail them afresh. It happened that although it had been raining for months and the river was high, now that a few houses of the Spanish settlement had been put up and the admiral was all set to leave for Spain, it stopped raining. What did this mean? Although it might usually have meant good weather, it was an awful situation for the Spaniards who saw the water level of the River Belén go down, leaving the caravels which were about to sail for Spain, trapped in the basin of the river. For they could not sail over the reef. Ferdinand Columbus wrote: 'We had nothing left to do but to pray God for rain as formerly we had prayed for fair weather.'

It might have also been coincidental that the Guaymis at last began to react to what the strangers had been doing to them. Stealthily, the Spaniards had been finding their way into the villages and extorting gold by force of arms. The Guaymis had had enough of this. They had made their guests as welcome as they possibly could, supplying food and every other comfort that the Spaniards could have wanted. They had given them permission to explore the rivers, and had even led them to the mines of gold. But instead of returning this kindness with courtesy the strangers were inflicting all sorts of indignities upon them: seizing their gold, destroying their property, violating their women, and now to show that these atrocious events were not just for a short time, the Spaniards were constructing a settlement so that they would be here always.

The fleet and the settlement began receiving clandestine visits from small groups of Guaymis, armed for war, who told the Spaniards that they were assembling to attack the people of a nearby province called Cobraba Aurira, with whom there was enmity. One of the Spaniards, Diego Méndez, felt uneasy about this. He did not believe their story, and went to Columbus. 'Sir', he said, 'These warriors who are passing up and down are not really preparing to make war on any one but us. I think what they are preparing to do is to burn our ships and kill every one of us.' Columbus asked him what he felt was the best way to prevent this. Diego Méndez said he would row up the coast towards Veragua to see if he could find their headquarters, to see what they were really doing. He did not even get as far as half a league when he saw about a thousand warriors together and seemingly ready for battle. He bravely got out of the boat and went to the shore alone to talk with them. Maybe he knew a little of the language for he was able to make himself understood. He told them that he wanted to go and fight on their side. But they made many excuses to the effect that it was not necessary. So he went back to the boat and remained all night looking at them. This made them change their plans, and on that same night they all returned to Veragua. Diego Méndez went back and reported to the admiral, who found the news very troubling, for he did not want to go back to Spain and leave a colony in danger behind him. Navidad was still too fresh in his mind. Columbus told Diego Méndez that since he did not have a force to adquately defend the new colony he was anxious to find out what really was the intention of these people. Then Diego Méndez decided boldly to go up to the headwaters of the Veragua River to see the cacique himself, and despite all persuasion not to risk his life in that way, he insisted on going. Accompanied by Rodrigo de Escobar, Diego Méndez rowed up the Veragua River towards the village of the cacique. Knowing that under normal circumstances he would not get very far, if indeed he was allowed to reach the village, he pretended that he was a doctor who had come to cure the cacique's bad leg. Believing this ruse the guards allowed him to go into the 'palace' of the cacique of that dangerous tribe. Years later, Méndez wrote: 'They suffered me to proceed to the seat of royalty, which was situated on a little plateau with a large square surrounded by about three hundred heads of warriors they had killed in battle.' His presence caused a furore and the cacique's son came out and forbade the stranger to enter. Diego Méndez wrote: 'I took out a comb, a pair of scissors, and a mirror, and then caused Escobar, my companion, to comb my hair and then cut it off.' This amazed the onlookers, and the cacique's son, who was so belligerent before, became very soft and reasonable. Diego, famished from the long journey up the River Veragua, then asked the cacique's son to bring food, which was done right away, and when the Spaniards had eaten they took their leave of the cacique's village and returned to their ships.

If that was all, then it would be difficult to see how Diego Méndez could have got clarification regarding whether the warriors intended to attack. But the next day Columbus called Diego Méndez and asked him what he thought should be done. Diego's advice was that the Spaniards should go and capture the cacique and all his high assistants, and in that way they would be able to subjugate the masses of the people. Columbus said he was of the identical opinion, and he arranged that his brother Bartholomew and Diego Méndez along with eighty armed men should go and carry out the deed. In his account, Diego Méndez said, 'And we went, and God gave us such good fortune that we seized the cacique and most of his captains, and wives and sons, and grandsons, with all the princes of his race, and sending them to the ships, thus captured, the cacique managed to escape from the slight grip of the man who was holding him, something that was to cause us a lot of hurt.'

Just around the time of this despicable act by the Spaniards it began raining very heavily, causing a great flood, and this enabled Columbus to draw the ships out over the reefs in order to get to sea and proceed to Spain. He decided to leave Diego behind to defend the fort, now that the warriors were completely demoralised. Columbus put together a force of seventy men for Diego, as well as the greater part of the stock of biscuits, wine, oil, and vinegar.

The admiral had hardly lifted anchor when the much feared action came. Diego Méndez was on shore with about twenty men when a great number of warriors (he said they were about 400) bore down on the Spaniards. They were armed with cross-bows and arrows, and they rent the air with shrieks and war-cries. They were just about an arrow-shot away. Suddenly came a shower of arrows 'thick as hail,' and some of the warriors left the group and rushed the Spaniards with clubs. This marked a turning point. The warriors apparently did not know the deadliness of steel, and the Spaniards literally cut them down. Arms and legs were severed and several of the assailants got killed on the spot. In that frightening battle the Spaniards lost seven of their seventy men, while they killed nine or ten of the men with clubs.

Columbus, looking out from the ship and noticing the battle on shore, did not leave. When the fight was over, Diego Tristan, a captain on the *Capitana*, came ashore with the ships' boats to take some final casks of water for the voyage. Diego Méndez said: 'Nothwithstanding I advised and warned him not to go, he would not listen to me, and against my wishes went up the river with the two boats and 12 men. Whereupon the natives attacked him and killed him as well as the 12 men he had with him, save one who escaped by swimming and brought us the news.' The warriors then took the boats and broke them up in pieces, which was a great blow to the Spaniards, for Columbus was out at sea, without any boats, and some of his men were on shore without any means of getting to him. And with all that, the warriors never ceased to harrass them, at every instant howling exultantly, considering that the Spaniards were already defeated.

In the face of all this it seemed foolhardy for the comparatively few Spaniards to remain thinking they could defend the fort. There was nothing to do but to abandon the new colony. The *Gallega* had been left for Diego Méndez. The big problem now was that with the ceasing of the rains the *Gallega* could not be got over the river-bar.

Columbus, who saw all this from the *Capitana* and who had had his misgivings in sending Diego Tristan for water, began to get worried. The *Capitana* was anchored some distance from the shore but the admiral seemed to have realised that there was further unrest. The failure of Captain Diego Tristan to return filled him with misgiving. More than that he noticed fighting was still going on and he thought all the Spaniards were being annihilated. He could not go back to shore because he did not have a sufficient force, and even if he did, what about the boats?

He wrote: 'I climbed to the highest part of the ship, and in a fearful voice cried out for help to Your Highnesses war captains in every direction, but none replied.'

From this it could be guessed that Columbus himself was not too well. He was suffering from a malarial fever, and this with the constant worry and nervous strain over Veragua, had rendered him delirious. Groaning with exhaustion he fell into a state of semi-sleep, and heard a voice, quite likely his own, telling him: 'O fool and slow to believe and serve thy God . . . What more did he do for Moses, or for David his servant, than for thee? From thy birth he had ever held thee in special charge. When he saw thee arrive at man's estate, marvellously did he cause thy name to resound over the earth. The Indias, so rich a portion of the world, he gave thee for thine own . . .'

Columbus' agony and delirium had to await four further days during which time Diego Méndez and his company of men – reduced to sixty-three – strove to keep off the warriors by frightening them with the blasting of powder and the firing of canon-balls. Also, during this time Diego was putting a crucial plan into action. He wrote: 'I caused several bags to be made out of the sails of one of the vessels which we had remaining on shore, and into them I put our biscuits. I then took two canoes and secured them together with sticks across the tops, and after loading them with the biscuits, the wine, and the oil and vinegar, I fastened them together with a rope and had them towed along the sea while it was calm, so that in seven trips we contrived to get all of it to the ships. The men were also carried over a few at a time. Meanwhile I remained with five men to the last, and at night I put to sea with the last boatful.'

Columbus embraced Diego Méndez for what he saw as an act of great heroism. It was hard for Diego to abandon Santa Maria de Belén but it was the only sensible thing to do. Columbus gave Diego Méndez the captaincy of the *Capitana* in place of Diego Tristan, who lost his life, and he said that he was putting him in charge of all the crew for the entire voyage.

Before Diego Méndez came back to the ships something happened that is worth remarking. The people who the Spaniards had captured in the Veragua raid, and who were in their prison aboard the *Santiago* had become extremely restive. They were kept below the deck, with the hatch cover fastened down by a chain, and some of the captives, managing to lift the hatch cover, escaped on deck and plunged into the sea to swim to shore. The watch then secured the hatch, but when daylight came and the hatch was removed to give the other captives air, the seamen were shocked at what they saw. The remaining captives, who included women, had got ropes from the hold and had hung themselves. They had been so determined, that in the absence of sufficient head-room, they had bent their knees, in order to help the swing of death.

With all the troubles and disasters behind them, the fleet, now reduced to three ships, set sail from this part of the 'Indias' on Easter night, 16th April 1503. Columbus was heading in the direction of Española, at which place he wanted to have some repairs to the ships carried out, and then he would make for Spain. The ships were in alarming condition, with water coming through holes bored by ship-worms. In fact they had to abandon one of them after going just about one hundred miles, and so they had just two ships now. Facing the wide open sea, and in utmost danger, they sailed for thirty-five days, and it must have been the strangest and most uninspired piece of navigation Christopher Columbus had ever done, for at the end of those thirty-five days, seeing a coast and feeling sure they had reached Spain, they pulled in to shore and noticed that they had landed at a point on the southern coast of Cuba. It could well have been that this was another ruse Columbus tried on the crew, who were eager to get back to Spain, for it is almost unbelievable he could have made such a mistake. Anyway, where they landed was about the middle of Cuba's long southern shore, where the city of Trinidad can be found today. The strangers did not stay in Cuba – the accounts do not say why – but left it for Jamaica, where they drove the two remaining ships on shore, because of the complete uselessness of both vessels at this stage. Water was coming into them as if the bottoms were sieves. It was almost a miracle that they had not gone under with all hands. Now at least, with the sailors marooned on this beach, the ships could be useful as a home until rescue came.

The beaching of the *Capitana* and the *Santiago* was not so easily done as said. It was laborious work. First the heavy stores had to be taken ashore, and the stone ballast thrown overboard. Each ship had to be pulled a little on shore by means of a winch. Then it had to be bailed out dry. Then there was the hard work of pulling the craft as far as possible onto the beach taking advantage of the high tide. The seamen could not have enjoyed doing this twice – once for each ship.

The marooned seamen converted the ships into two great cabins with separate little cabins on deck, their roofs thatched with palms. The men placed artillery all around so that they could beat off any attack. This place would be their residence until the natives wiped them out or until a miracle happened to deliver them.

They must have been very watchful because those who had been on past voyages would have remembered that they had had hostile greetings whenever they had landed on Jamaica. Their constant fear now was that the vessels, with their thatched roofs, might be set on fire. This could very easily be done under the cover of night. Also it was clear that the Spaniards did not trust the native peoples, for they themselves had left such a trail of cruelty and destruction in their path that it was difficult for them to imagine anyone could leave them alone.

The place of the beached ships made an excellent fort and an excellent home under the circumstances. It was on a hill and the Spaniards commanded the view all around. Ferdinand Columbus, who was now fifteen, described it as no mean fort. Also, there were two good streams of fresh water nearby, and there was a large village called Maima about half a mile away. Columbus' name for this place – a name he had given since the second voyage – was Santa Gloria.

The last of the biscuits and wine were given out while there, and with the Spaniards desperate for food, Diego Méndez, the bravest and boldest among Columbus' men, as well as the man Columbus had put in overall charge of the fleet, took a sword in his hand, and accompanied by three of the crew, advanced into the island. Fortunately the villagers they met were friendly or there could easily have been four Spaniards less. But the

Fig.55   Indians making bread, from Benzoni's *Historia del Mondo Nuovo,* 1563

villagers were not only pleasant but generous, and gave the Spaniards food with great goodwill. Diego Méndez then entered into an agreement with a cacique that his people supply a daily amount of cassava bread and fish and other provisions and bring these to the ships daily, and that they be paid right there in blue beads, combs, knives, fish-hooks, hawk's bells, and other such articles.

For Diego Méndez, this was not enough. He wrote: 'I went further on, and came to a great cacique called Huareo, living in a place which is now called Melilla, 13 leagues from where the ships lay. I was very well received by him. He gave me plenty to eat, and ordered all his subjects to bring together in the course of three days a great quantity of provisions – which they did, and laid them before him, whereupon I paid them to his full satisfaction. I made an agreement with him that they should furnish a constant supply.'

It would seem that in going about the country and making such agreements Diego Méndez was not simply assuring that the Spaniards would have enough food, for if the agreements were kept up they would already be having much too much. It would seem that in making these agreements Diego was assuring that the Spaniards, completely marooned in Jamaica, would be protected by the various 'peace treaties', which the agreements amounted to. He went to almost every important cacique of the island, who no doubt felt even more important to have such an agreement, and elated to have so much of hawk's bells, blue beads, fish-hooks, and knives. He asked Huareo to give him two men to go with him to the extremity of the island, one to carry the hammock in which he slept, the other to carry the food.

Huareo gave him these two persons and he set off for the eastern end of the island. There he met a cacique called Ameyro, to whom he became very close. He said, 'I gave him my name, and I took his, which, among them, is regarded as

Fig.56   An Indian hammock tied between two trees, from Oviedo's *La hystoria generale de las Indias,* 1547

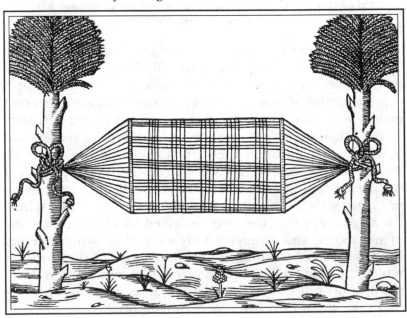

great brotherly attachment.' Diego Méndez bought a very beautiful canoe from this cacique, and gave him in exchange a fine brass helmet, a gown, and a shirt. The two persons that Huareo had sent with him to bear the hammock and the food must have taken their leave, for Diego Méndez, desiring to return in the canoe, asked Cacique Ameyro, his friend, for six men to help in guiding the canoe. With the six men Diego reached Santa Gloria, the place of the beached caravels, and when Columbus saw him he was so moved that he embraced and kissed him, according to Diego Méndez. Columbus, who must have worried about this bold and determined soldier, and must have wondered what had become of him, offered up thanks to God for having given him back. The men also rejoiced to see Diego, for thanks to the arrangements he had made, there was now more than enough food to feed the crew Columbus had with him.

However, after the passage of ten days, during which Columbus eyed the villagers very closely, he called Diego aside and said: 'Diego, none of these sailors I have with me realise what peril we are in, except myself and you. We are in danger because we are very few, and these savage Indians are very fickle, and if they take it into their heads to come and burn us up in our two ships covered with straw, they could do this very easily by setting fire to them from the land side.'

Then he touched on the arrangements to supply food, arrangements which Diego went to so much trouble to make, and to which the caciques had agreed with so much goodwill. Columbus said, 'They could suddenly decide they don't wish to do that, and don't be surprised if tomorrow morning no food comes. In such a case we are in no position to take it by force, and we shall have to agree to their terms.'

Then Columbus made a suggestion. As it was, they had no ships, and they could not remain there forever. His suggestion was that someone should go out to sea in that excellent canoe that Diego had purchased and try and make his way to Haiti and there purchase a vessel from the authorities and let it come for them at Santa Gloria in order that they might escape from the extremely dangerous position in which they found themselves.

Diego Méndez replied that to make the trip from Jamaica to Haiti in such a small canoe was not only difficult but impossible. He said among the sailors he did not know a single person who would be so rash as to attempt to cover over 100 miles in waters that were always so wild and turbulent.

Columbus did not agree with him that this would be impossible. Then looking him in the eye Columbus told him straight, 'You are the man to go. You are the person to undertake this enterprise'.

Diego said, with resignation, 'My Lord, I have many times put my life in danger to save yours and the lives of those you have with you. And I am still here. And remember there have been a lot of murmurings amongst the seamen that you give missions of honour to me, while there are others who could do them just as well. So my opinion is that your lordship should summon all the men and put this proposal to them and see if any of them would accept it – which I doubt very much. And if no one accepts it. I shall risk my life again, as I have done so many times before.'

The next day Columbus called the men together and put the proposal to them. At first they were silent, they could not believe it. Then some of them said it was out of the question even to speak of such a thing. It was an impossible mission. Nobody could make that crossing, they said.

Then Diego Méndez rose and said, 'My Lord, I have only one life, no more. But I am willing to risk it to serve you now, and for the welfare of all those you have with you here.'

The following day he prepared his canoe. He put on a false keel, he greased, caulked the grooves with pitch, nailed some boards on the poop to keep off sea-water, and he put up a mast and affixed a sail to it. He put in the necessary provisions, then he selected a Spaniard to go with him, as well as six natives of the place – making the company eight people, which was as many as the boat would hold. He then sailed up the coast to the eastern extremity of the island, which, according to Ferdinand Columbus, was called Aramaquique. This place was just over a hundred miles from Santa Gloria.

While Diego Méndez was preparing his boat for the voyage Columbus was hastily writing a letter to the king and queen of Spain, a letter which he wanted to send directly by Diego Méndez, providing that Diego Méndez could reach Santo Domingo safely, from where he would go on to Spain. In the letter Columbus does not speak of his predicament so much as complains of the treatment he has suffered in the past by the royal officials. He ends by saying: 'I came to serve [Your Highnesses] at the age of 28, and now I have no hair upon me that is not white, and my body is infirm and exhausted. All that was left to me and to my brothers has been taken away and sold, even the cloak that I wore, to my great dishonour. It is believed that this was not done by your royal command. The restitution of my honour and losses, and the punishment of those who have inflicted them, of those who plundered me of my pearls, and who have disparaged my Admiral's privileges, will redound to the honour of your royal dignity.'

At the very end of the letter Columbus says: 'I came to Your Highnesses with honest purpose and sincere zeal, and I do not speak falsely. I humbly beg Your Highnesses that if it pleases God to remove me hence, you will aid me to go to Rome and on other pilgrimages. May the Holy Trinity guard and increase your lives and high estate.'

He is most meticulous in putting the date: 'Done in the Indias, in the island of Jamaica, on the seventh of July, in the year one thousand five hundred and three.'

One thing that can be noticed by the letter is that Columbus knew he was not going to find death at Santa Gloria. Another thing is the great contradiction throughout: the saintly Columbus who wishes to go on pilgrimages to Rome, and the Columbus who thought nothing of capturing caciques, seizing their wives and children, even butchering them, and laying waste their property. The expedition at Veragua is just one example to cite.

At that moment Columbus' brave crewman Diego Méndez, was preparing to dare the crossing to Haiti. Just before he took off from Aramaquique a horde of villagers gathered with the intention of killing him, but he managed to slip them and went back to the beached caravels, which he got to after fifteen days sailing, which would indicate that the sea was very wayward and turbulent. On arrival Diego went to Columbus and told him of all that had happened. He wrote afterwards: 'His lordship was very joyful at my arrival and asked me if I would recommence my voyage. I told him I would if I could take some men to be with me to protect me at the extremity of the island until I could find a fair opportunity of putting to sea and escaping those pirates.'

Columbus gave him seventy men, led by his brother Bartholomew. They were to protect him at the other end of the island until he had put to sea and were to remain there for three days after his departure. Arriving there, he waited four days until the sea became calm enough. He declared: 'I then commended myself to God and to Our Lady of Antigua, and was at sea five days and four nights without laying down the oars from my hand, but continued steering the canoe, while my companions rowed. It pleased God that at the end of five days I reached the Island of Española at Cape San

Fig.57   An Indian canoe, from Benzoni's *Historia del Mondo Nuovo,* 1563

Miguel.' That was the end of July 1503.

Diego Méndez does not tell us that he was accompanied on that crossing by another big canoe, commanded by Bartolomeo Fieschi. This was the Genoese known to the Columbus family, and who had been recruited in Seville as captain of the *Vizcaíña*. It had been agreed that Méndez and Fieschi should each take six Spaniards and ten natives in the hope that at least one of the canoes would reach Haiti. In case that both succeeded in reaching Haiti, Diego Méndez was to press on to Santo Domingo to arrange a rescue ship, then proceed to Spain with the letter, and Fieschi would return to Jamaica with the news.

The fact that both canoes managed to arrive at Haiti was one of the most outstanding pieces of navigation on the fourth voyage. It was also a case of great luck. Considering the size of the canoes and the wild waters they had to confront over a distance of about 110 miles it was a mission that seemed impossible, as Columbus' men had felt, and as Diego Méndez himself had declared. The crossing itself was far from comfortable and the extraordinary thing about it was the fact that the natives wilted much more than the strangers. Drinking water which the native rowers had brought seemed to have been spilled into the sea and on the second day out these rowers were so thirsty that one of them died. The others had to just lie on the bottom of the canoe, weak and bemused. On the third night, they came to Nevassa, a little islet on the way, and there they landed and searched for fresh water in the hollows of rocks. Whether that water was contaminated by sulphur or other properties one does not know, but, recalling the incident, Ferdinand Columbus said some of the natives drank so much that they died, while other natives 'got desperate distempers'. So they were completely useless. The rest of the crew had to work so hard during the voyage that they were exhausted onto death. They never stopped rowing for fear that the winds and currents would take their canoe off course, and it need not be said that they had had no sleep over the five days and four nights. Fortunately, the people at Cape Tiburon (referred to by Diego Méndez as Cape San Miguel) were of a very peaceable and friendly nature, for the adventurers could hardly stand, let alone fight. These people brought a lot to eat and drink, and the countryside itself was extremely charming to look at. Diego Méndez said he remained there two days resting.

When he recovered nobody would go on with him to Santo Domingo so he took six of the inhabitants of Cape Tiburon to proceed on the journey. Fieschi decided to return right away but neither the natives who had crossed with him nor his own countrymen wanted to risk the terrible ordeal of the crossing for a second time.

Meanwhile Diego Méndez had set off on his quest for Santo Domingo, with the journey at that point being about 400 miles long. Sailing eastwardly for about 240 miles took him to Azoa, at which place the Spanish Commander, Gallego, told him that the governor, Nicolas de Ovando, had gone on an expedition from Santo Domingo to subdue the province of Xaragua, which was about 150 miles away. Méndez left his canoe and took the road to Xaragua, where he met the governor. But the governor, who must have been secretly happy to hear that Columbus was marooned in Jamaica, and no doubt counting on his dying soon, detained Diego Méndez with him for seven months while he did official business. And this official business was 'until he had burned and hanged 84 caciques, including Anacoana, the sovereign mistress of the island . . .' to quote from Diego's account. When the official business was over and the expedition completed, Diego Méndez covered over 200 miles on foot to Santo Domingo, and there waited two months on the arrival of ships from Spain. The Crown had a small caravel in port but Ovando would not let him use it. Shortly afterwards three ships arrived, and Méndez bought one of them, filled it with provisions, bread, wine, meat, hogs, sheep, and fruit, and despatched it over to the place where the admiral was staying – that is, the place of the beached caravels at Santa Gloria, Jamaica. He expected the admiral to come over with his men in the vessel to Santo Domingo, and from there leave for Spain. From the time of his departure from Santa Gloria, the place of the beached caravels, to that moment, it was almost a year.

Nothing was heard of Fieschi and his return to Santa Gloria

in the canoe. Apparently he found it impossible to obtain rowers to go with him. But he did not perish, for we see him in Spain years later.

As to Diego Méndez, he went on straight to Spain, carrying out Columbus' orders. He ended this part of the account by disclosing: 'I myself went on in advance in the two other ships, in order to give an account to the king and queen of all that had occurred on this voyage.'

Meanwhile, at Santa Gloria there arose the threat of mutiny. After waiting for about a year without seeing a ship come the men grew uneasy. They were already very much irked and discontented by the admiral seeking to confine them to the beached caravels, and in fact they were ripe for mischief. And a great amount of mischief was now being stirred up by the brothers Porras.

Francisco Porras, a captain, was one of the officers on the *Santiago* and his brother Diego was the representative of the Crown, one whose main duty was to keep a check on the gold being brought aboardship. Since so little gold was got, he had been all but completely idle on the voyage. Francisco had felt all along that Columbus had his own private reasons for marooning himself, that he had lost favour with Ovando and could not go to Haiti. But did that mean, he thought, that the rest of the men must perish here, maybe massacred by the native warriors?

The hundred or so men and boys formed two opposing camps. About half of them determined to brave the waves to Haiti however they could, led by the Porras brothers; and the other half retained their loyalty to the admiral. It was the close of the year 1503, and this Christmas Day was a very cheerless one, there being not even a little wine to celebrate, and as could be imagined, not even a semblance of Spanish food. New Year's Day was just as bad. However, for the anti-Columbus faction, New Year's Day must have been spent with a certain degree of nervousness for the Porras brothers had set their moment of action for the following day. That next morning, 2nd January 1504, Francisco Porras entered the admiral's room brusquely and asked him if he meant to keep them there until they perished. Columbus replied: 'I want to go home as much as anyone. But how can we leave without a ship?'

Porras declared: 'There's no more time to talk. Embark with us or stay with God!'

At this point the men supporting Francisco were within earshot. Francisco cried: 'To Castile. Who will follow me?'

They all shouted: 'We are with you!' And in a general commotion they took possession of various parts of the ship.

A quarrel followed, with Columbus, who was down with arthritis, tottering out of his room, and according to one account he would certainly have been murdered had not some of his devoted servants got hold of him and forced him back. His brother Bartholomew came running out with a lance, but again the admiral's servants pulled it away from him and pushed him into his brother's room. Then they entreated Porras to go in peace, do whatever he wanted, but commit no murder.

The mutineers got into ten canoes, which had been tied to the ships, and some who were not even in the mutiny went with them. They sailed eastwardly along the coast, stopping now and again at native villages to seize things from them, saying that the admiral would pay. At the eastern end of the island they waited on the weather and set off for Haiti when they saw that it looked calm. But as they set off the typical January turbulence rose suddenly. They threw everything overboard to prevent the canoes from sinking, and after throwing out the goods, they threw out some of the native rowers, lopping off the arms of those who clung on to the canoes. They then changed direction and made the native rowers head for the easternmost village, spending a month there and living off the native Jamaicans. While there they made two more attempts to cross and both attempts failed. In the end they abandoned their canoes and headed overland for Santa Gloria. As they passed through villages on their way back they left a trail of dissatisfaction, distress, and injury. When they reached Santa Gloria they set up a camp in the region of the beached caravels.

Not only did things go bad with Columbus so far as the loyalty of the Spaniards were concerned, but things also went awry as far as the inhabitants of Jamaica were concerned. They began to go back on the promises they had so faithfully made to supply food.

The reason for this was not simply that they were fickle, as the Spaniards loved to make out. True, they changed their minds and their moods very quickly, but often this was because of the treatment meted out to them. Wherever the Spaniards had been in these 'Indias' they had unjustifiably taken the sword to the inhabitants. And this was even after acts of great kindness. Outstanding examples to be recalled would be Haiti on the first and second voyages, and Veragua on this the fourth voyage, where they often went on the rampage kidnapping caciques, seizing the women, capturing anything that looked like gold, looting, plundering, and laying waste.

So it was not surprising that the contract to bring food to the Spaniards at Santa Gloria was not being honoured in the same way as before. The Spaniards were honourable in their payments for these services – the payment, of course, being in lace points, brass rings, hawks' bells, glass beads and the like. What may have been happening, too, was that, figuratively speaking, the shine on this useless merchandise was beginning to wear off. The inhabitants were sufficiently used to them and these articles were no longer novelties. In any case by now they must have had so much that they probably wanted no more.

The fact was that the supply of food was dwindling daily, and the Spaniards were facing starvation. Of course, had it been other times when they had a lot more men, and a great deal more gunpowder, they would have gone and ransacked the villages and taken food, but doing that now would be inviting easy massacre.

What was there to be done to get more food? Columbus, as resourceful and crafty as always, summoned the caciques to meet him at a conference on the night of 29th February. The date then was 26th February, and Columbus thought of the scheme just at the right moment, for 29th February, 1504, was going to be a most crucial date. One of the books that Columbus had with him on the voyage and which he consulted as often as he consulted the Bible was *Ephemerides*, a book by Johannes Muller (Regiomontanus) that predicted eclipses of the sun and moon for thirty-two years (1475 – 1506). It happened that a total eclipse of the moon was predicted to take place on 29th February, 1504, just a matter of three nights ahead.

When the caciques assembled on the *Capitana* that night Columbus told them that the Spaniards had come to Jamaica by the direct command of God, who was at their home in heaven. He said God rewarded the good and punished the wicked. He said even some of those who had themselves come from heaven, God punished sometimes, like Porras and his men, with whom God was angry, and did not let cross over to Haiti in the canoes. He told the caciques that God had noticed that they, the native peoples, were not dutiful in supplying food and provisions to the children of heaven and that God was very angry and was going to show them that very night signs of the vengeance he was going to take on them. The admiral then called on the caciques to watch the rising of the moon. He declared: 'It will be red and terrible and covered with blood. And this is the sign of the destruction that will befall your people.'

Ferdinand Columbus then describes what happened next. He said the caciques departed, some in fear and others scoffing. But he said the caciques took heed when the moon began to rise red and bloody-looking, and when they saw this they became so frightened 'that with great howling and lamentation they came running from every direction to the ships, laden with provisions, begging the admiral to intercede with God on their behalf by all means, that He might not visit his wrath upon them, promising for the future diligently to furnish all that they stood in need of.'

Ferdinand goes on: 'To this the Admiral replied that he wished to converse somewhat with God, and he retired while the eclipse lasted, they all the while crying out to him to aid them. And when the Admiral observed that the eclipse had reached its limit and that the moon would soon shine forth as normally, he came out of his cabin saying that he had talked with God and intervened on their behalf, and he had promised God, in their name, that they would be kind to the Christians from now on. Through him, God had pardoned them, the

Admiral told them, and that the sign of the pardon would be the wrath and blood passing away from the moon and the moon shining normally. They kept rendering thanks to the Admiral until the eclipse ended. From that time forward they always took care to provide what we had need of.'

That was perhaps the most effective and dramatic hoax that Columbus had brought off on any of the voyages. When he had retired to his cabin, with the caciques howling outside, he had engaged in something much more within his reach than conversing with God. He was using the eclipse to fix the longitude of Jamaica in relation to the longitude of Spain. This gifted admiral wrote down his findings thus: 'Thursday 29th February, 1504, I being in the Indias on the Island of Jamaica, in the harbour called Santa Gloria, which is almost in the middle of the island on the north side, there was an eclipse of the moon, and as the beginning thereof was before the sun set, I could only note the end of it . . .'

But using an estimate as to what time the eclipse had begun, and reckoning what time it actually ended, he concluded: 'The difference between the middle of the Island of Jamaica in the Indias and the Island of Cadiz in Spain is seven hours and fifteen minutes.' Actually it was five hours and a few minutes, but given what Columbus had to work with, it was a magnificent effort.

But from astronomy to superstition: in reality the eclipse had more bad portents for the Spaniards than for the caciques and other inhabitants of Jamaica, for shortly after it took place the affairs of the Spaniards became radically worse. Food was being supplied all right; more food than they could use. But the question of leaving Jamaica as well as the question of the relationship between the two groups of Spaniards showed that matters were very much in disarray. It was March 1504, more than eight months since Diego Méndez and Bartolomeo Fieschi had left, when a small caravel appeared at Santa Gloria. But it was not a caravel sent by Diego Méndez. This caravel was sent by Governor Ovando, and it was not to collect the admiral and his men but apparently just to observe what was happening to Ovando's hated enemy, Columbus, and report. Still, the captain of the caravel, who was Deigo de Escobar, had the good grace to go aboard the beached *Capitana* and greet the admiral before setting sail that very evening. He gave Columbus two casks of wine and a slab of salt pork, as presents coming from Governor Ovando, but it is very doubtful that Ovando had sent Columbus anything. Far from being so generous to Columbus, one is inclined to join Las Casas in his belief that Ovando had despatched Diego de Escobar to see if Columbus was dead. It might be recalled that Diego de Escobar himself had rebelled against Columbus in Haiti during the period of the second voyage, but this captain was certainly not as bitter as Ovando was. When the Escobar vessel left that evening Columbus sought to ease the sharp disappointment of the marooned Spaniards by saying Diego's vessel was too small to take everybody, and that he felt they should all wait until a bigger one was sent. Anyway, one piece of information that was of great importance to all, and a major relief to the admiral, was the following: Diego Méndez had reached Española safely and would send a rescue party as soon as he could obtain a ship. This information was obviously sent while Diego Méndez was still awaiting a caravel at Santo Domingo.

The departure of the Escobar caravel might have been the most depressing event of that period for the seamen, but further dramatic and eventful things were in the offing. The two groups of Spaniards, those loyal to Columbus and the rebels under Francisco de Porras, were not reconciled, and Columbus was never happy about this. Apart from the fact that Porras' men were roaming the villages committing wanton and cruel acts, making life tougher for the Spaniards in general, Columbus did not want the natives of Jamaica to see that the 'Children from Heaven' could not agree among themselves. So the big-hearted admiral sent a slice of Ovando's salted pork to Porras' camp, as a peace offering, and at the same time announced a general pardon for all. Porras, realising that Columbus was sueing for peace, now began making big and unreasonable demands. The parley was broken off, but the rebels, getting the impression that Columbus wanted peace because the loyalists were in a bad way, decided to march on Santa Gloria. They reached Maima on 19th May and were in sight of the beached ships. Bartholomew Columbus struck out to meet them with fifty armed men. The two sides clashed at Maima, and this may have been to the admiral's great distress. He had not wanted the inhabitants to see the Spaniards divided, but now great crowds were being gleefully entertained by watching the Spaniards desperately locked in battle against each other, thrusting, cutting, attempting to slice up each other with their swords. However, only one man was actually killed, and the battle saw the loyalists carrying the day. Francisco de Porras was captured and put in irons.

That was precisely the time that Diego Méndez was able to fit out his rescue ship. This was two months after he had arrived in Santo Domingo, having been detained seven months by Ovando at Xaragua, and it was eleven months since he had set off from Santa Gloria.

Diego Méndez had had to await vessels coming from Spain and after he had been in Santo Domingo two months a fleet of three caravels arrived. Méndez chartered what was perhaps the smallest caravel (maybe what his means could afford) stocked it with enough food, and sent it to Jamaica captained by Diego de Salcedo. Then, as Columbus had commanded, he went on to Spain to deliver letters to the sovereign.

The brave little rescue caravel duly arrived at Santa Gloria, and the joy and relief of the marooned men could hardly have been described. Joy, too, must have been the sentiment of the inhabitants of Jamaica. After all, it had been many, many moons since they had been able to live their own normal lives. Of course, although they did not know it, this was only the end of the first chapter of a long and terrible history. Their lives were never to be the same again.

The caravel of rescue left Santa Gloria on 29th June 1504, and the 'Admiral of the Ocean Sea' was again where he belonged – on the ocean sea. All the men left behind were with him, and they numbered about one hundred. They had been marooned in Jamaica one year and four days, having beached the *Capitana* and the *Santiago* on 25th June, 1503.

The little rescue caravel was not a stout vessel and it was reported that the sailors had difficulty in keeping her afloat. There were several defects about it, and its sails were rotten and its main-mast was not functioning well. It took an

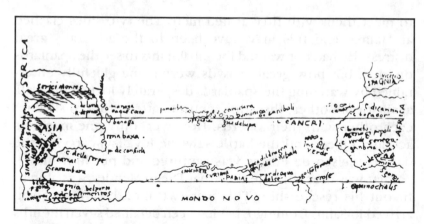

Fig.58   The 'New World' as Columbus saw it after four voyages

incredibly long time to reach Santo Domingo – six weeks and a few days. Here in Santo Domingo Columbus was to see hypocrisy at its most amazing. But happy hypocrisy: it was Ovando who expressed great joy at seeing Columbus, embraced him, and took him into his own house. However, he never punished the Porras brothers for their treachery.

Columbus remained another three months at Santo Domingo for it was not until 12th September 1504 that he was able to sail for Spain. His brother Bartholomew and his son Ferdinand embarked with him, along with twenty-two others of his men. Most of the survivors preferred to stay in Haiti. A few of these, maybe former mutineers who did not wish to sail with Columbus, sailed to Spain on the very unseaworthy little caravel that had rescued them from Jamaica. The Porras brothers were in that vessel.

Columbus' homeward vessel was not very good either. In chartering it he was chartering a certain amount of trouble and it was good for all on the ship that Christopher Columbus and Bartholomew Columbus together could sail almost anything, especially with the help of Ferdinand Columbus, now a young man of sixteen. The Columbus caravel, bearing the three Columbus stalwarts of the fourth voyage, reached the Spanish port of San Lucar de Barrameda on 7th November 1504. This was two and a half years since the admiral had set sail on the fourth voyage.

EPILOGUE
Home Again in Spain

It was rather strange, and it went down hard with Columbus, that after having suffered so much he was not even invited to court to tell his story. In fact he was completely ignored. True, Columbus, though he was an excellent mariner, was a tiresome complainer, and it would not have been surprising if the sovereigns had been trying to avoid this.

Maybe one should say 'the sovereign', for Queen Isabella was seriously ill and therefore not in a position to decide. In fact it was her illness which was given as the excuse for Columbus not having been invited to court. Yet this was a great pity. For Isabella was on her death-bed, and having been such a great and tenacious friend of Columbus, and having seen him through and kept in close touch with all of his four voyages, it might have been moving to see her take her leave of him.

But alas, this was not to be. Less than three weeks after Columbus arrived from the 'Indias' Queen Isabella died. She died on 26th November 1504.

The death of Isabella the Catholic was the death of all Columbus' chances of redress, because she was the one who had ceaselessly fought for him and who in fact appeared to make decisions on his rights and privileges. But Columbus would have been a much happier man had he simply retired in contentment and proceeded to live out the rest of his days as a rich man. For there was no question that he was extremely rich now, what with all the 'tenth' and 'eighth' and 'third' parts that were set out in the Discovery Contract (and now bearing fruit), as well as a lot of gold the admiral had secured, including the great quantity he had obtained during his exploration of Veragua.

But he never ceased to ask for the restitution of his rights, some of them imaginary and fanciful, and he plagued his son Diego, who was now a bodyguard at court, to straighten out matters for him.

By the opening of 1505 letters from Columbus pressing the king to recognise his right to be Governor of Santo Domingo seem to have ceased, and there was a lessening in harsh words about Ovando and other men who had ill-used him, like Francisco de Bobadilla, who had perished in the storm. And indeed things had certainly changed, because there was no hint from the admiral about making another voyage. Columbus seems to have realised at last that enough was enough. The truth was that his body could not undertake another voyage to the 'Indias', and although what he had craved most of all was not another voyage of exploration but to be Governor of Santo Domingo, he knew that if the king was to finally give his assent to this he, Columbus, had not the strength to assume the post. Yet he was only fifty-four.

The queen's death must have seemed to Christopher Columbus, to his brother Bartholomew, and to his sons Diego and Ferdinand, to have made a much sharper difference than they had expected. For although gold from the 'Indias' was now regularly being sent to Spain, thanks to Ovando, the king never seemed to spare a thought for Columbus, nor did he seem to regard him as anything else but troublesome. All the little requests of Columbus to the king went unheeded. On one occasion, when Columbus wanted to make a cross-country journey, the king did grant him permission to ride a mule (the riding of mules at that time was forbidden) but there were no big favours. Eventually, though, a big favour did come, and this was in respect to Columbus' older son, Diego. Diego was twenty-five years old, and had had the noble title of 'Don' conferred upon him by the sovereigns. He was known at court as Don Diego Colón. Columbus had repeatedly asked for Diego to assume his title as admiral after his death, and in fact this was a 'right', as reflected in the Discovery Contract. But the king had never formally given his word on this. Diego, who had been left at court as a page-boy while his father made his four voyages, had grown into a magnificent young man, well-

Fig.59   Columbus' coat of arms

built, handsome, and well-mannered, and the king liked him. Now the king agreed to make him Admiral of the Ocean Sea and Governor-General of the Islands of the Sea, after his father's death.

But towards Columbus himself, some historians could be forgiven if they felt the king had grown vicious. For King Ferdinand went so far, in 1505, as to instruct Ovando to sell any 'moveable' property of Columbus in Haiti and send the money to the treasury, and any possession of Columbus sent to Spain was to be impounded to pay the admiral's debts. This was a secret order, and mercifully, Columbus never got to hear of it.

Columbus did meet the king face to face, the occasion being in May 1505. The admiral had set out on mule-back on a long journey to the court at Segovia in Old Castile.

There was apparently no warmth in the meeting. On Columbus' side it was not the same. 'Isabella querida' was not there. On the king's side the fact that Columbus' most stubborn champion was not beside him on the throne made it easier for him to be absolutely unyielding, although he was polite.

For Columbus could not miss the opportunity to bore and irritate the king by bringing up the question of his claims. Columbus must have seen meeting the king face to face as a 'golden' opportunity in every sense of the word. But it availed him nothing. The king's view was that if Columbus wanted to be meticulous about claims, then everything had to be considered, even his title as admiral, the question of his

Fig.60   Columbus before the Council at Salamanca

viceroyalty, etc. Columbus refused to have these arbitrated, from the point of view that they were his already, and were not in question. In the end there could be no discussion and Columbus got nothing.

This must have broken Columbus' heart, although, oddly enough, it does not seem to have made him bitter. The court moved to Salamanca, and then to Valladolid, and both times the great 'Admiral of the Ocean Sea' followed. But his fifty-four years sat very heavily upon him. All the toil and trouble against those raging seas, the encounter with mosquitoes and other vermin as he explored the 'Indias' in his search for gold, the storms and tempests that assailed him on his voyages, especially on this past one, when he was looking for the strait on the coast of Veragua, Chiriqui, Cariay. All this and the weight of those twelve months he was marooned at Jamaica: the physical and mental anguish of that period. These things had taken a heavy toll of his strength, and he was paying the dues now. The arthritis which had always assailed him on the fourth voyage was increasing rapidly. In fact, he must have wished he could have really talked personally with God, as he had led the caciques to believe at Santa Gloria on that night of the eclipse, for he felt he had done so much, and yet had to suffer so terribly. His attendants looked at him and their hearts were filled with grief.

On 19th May 1506, Christopher Columbus, always with a flair for the right moment, attended to his last will and testament. He bequeathed to Don Diego Colón all his property and privileges. This was the customary treatment towards the eldest son, but he also seemed to be remarkably fond of Don Diego. Many observers expected the favourite to be Ferdinand, who had always been at his side on the fourth voyage, and who worked manfully on his father's vessel, touching the heart of the admiral. However, it must be said that what distinguished Columbus during the voyages, was the closeness and affection that he had for all of his relatives. For instance, he often ended his letters to Ferdinand with the words: 'The father who loves thee more than himself.' Also, in moments of danger he would have easily given his life, not only for Ferdinand, but for either of his two brothers, indeed, especially for Bartholomew, who more than once risked his own life for the admiral.

So far as the making of the will was concerned, Columbus displayed a magnificent sense of timing. He attended to the making of the will on 19th May, and it was the very next day, 20th May that the end came. Bartholomew was absent, he was at the royal court, but the admiral's younger brother Diego, the sons, Don Diego Colón, and Ferdinand, were around the death-bed. Also there was the faithful and loyal Diego Méndez, as well as Bartholomeo Fieschi, the two who had manned the canoes which crossed from Jamaica to Haiti. These two great admirers of Columbus were on hand to see their master off on his final voyage. In addition there were a few domestics watching the admiral leave.

A priest was summoned and Columbus received the last sacrament. And then the final moment came. The man who in 1492 had set out on a golden quest, braving uncharted waters with rough men in his company, and encountering land he believed to be part of India, and in fact never knew how mistaken he was, had now taken his leave of this world. The extraordinary captain, maybe the greatest seaman in history; a man who had made the crossing a second time after returning

Fig.61   Sebastian Munster's map of the 'New World' in 1550

in 1493, and a third time, and a fourth, had departed, and was never ever going to be replaced. A good man, but far from being a saint – and in fact extremely cruel at times, as we have seen – he enabled the two sides of the world to know each other. The great irony is that despite all his work the name of the continent he came upon was given, inadvertently, to a keen but upstart seaman who sailed with him on the third voyage – Amerigo Vespucci. The continent was of course called America.

However, the name of Christopher Columbus will not be forgotten. For in 1492, with a heart filled with the golden quest, and counting on the much-advanced theory that the Earth was round, he sailed into the sunset and arrived on the shores of another world.

Bibliography

First Voyage

The Journal of Christopher Columbus The log of his first voyage presented by Bartholomew de las Casas, edited by Cecil Jane, Anthony Blond and The Orion Press, London 1960.

Life and Times of Columbus, Paul Hamlyn, London 1967

Christopher Columbus to Lord Robert Sanchez taken from *Selected Letters of Christopher Columbus*, by R.H. Major, Corinth Books, New York, 1961

Trinidad and Tobago Historical Society, Document No. 91 in *Documents of West Indian History,* by Dr Eric Williams, P.N.M. Publishing Company, Port-of-Spain, 1963

The History of the Life and Actions of the Admiral Christopher Columbus by his son Ferdinand Columbus, Rutgers University Press, New Jersey, 1959.

Admiral of the Ocean Sea by Samuel Eliot Morison, Little, Brown and Company, Boston, 1942.

Second Voyage

Report on the second voyage of Christopher Columbus by Dr Pedro Chanca (medical doctor to the fleet on the second voyage) taken from the volume *Selected Letters of Christopher Columbus* by R.H. Major, Corinth Books, New York, 1961.

Christopher Columbus, the Mariner and the Man by Jean Merrien, Odhams Press Ltd, London, 1958

Admiral of the Ocean Sea, by Samuel Eliot Morison, Little, Brown and Company, Boston, 1942.

Third Voyage

Columbus' account of the Third Voyage in a letter to the king and queen of Spain, quoted in R.H. Major's *Selected Letters of Christopher Columbus,* Corinth Books, New York, 1961.

The History of the Life and Actions of the Admiral Christopher Columbus by his son, Ferdinand Columbus, Rutgers University Press, New Jersey, 1959.

Fourth Voyage

Account from the last Will and Testament of Diego Méndez as quoted in *Selected Letters of Christopher Columbus* by R.H. Major, Corinth Books, New York, 1961.

The History of the Life and Actions of the Admiral Christopher Columbus by his son, Ferdinand Columbus, Rutgers University Press, New Jersey, 1959.

Admiral of the Ocean Sea by Samuel Eliot Morison, Little, Brown and Company, Boston, 1942.

Documents of West Indian History by Dr Eric Williams, P.N.M. Publishing Company, Port-of-Spain, 1963.

List of Island Names

Present name	Original name	Spanish/ Columbus' name
Antigua		Santa Maria de la Antigua
Cuba	Cuba	Juana
Dominica	Wy-tou-Koubouli	Dominica
Grenada		Asuncion
Guadeloupe	Kerukera	Santa Maria de Guadeloupe
Haiti and the Dominican Republic	Haiti, also Bohio	Española
Jamaica	Yamaye	Xamaica
Long Island	Samana (Bahamas)	Fernandina
Marie Galante	Ayay	Maria Galante
Martinique	Matinino	
Montserrat		Santa Maria de Montserrat
Nevis		San Martin
Puerto Rico	Borinquen	San Juan Bautista
Rum Cay		Santa Maria de Concepcion
Saba		San Cristóbal
St Christopher		San Jorge
St Croix	Ayay	Santa Cruz
St Eustatius		Santa Anastasia
St Lucia	Hewanorra	
St Vincent	Hairon	
Tobago	Tobaco	Bellaforma

Present name	Original name	Spanish/Columbus' name
Vieques	Vieques	Graciosa
Virgin Islands		Once Mil Virgenes
Watling Island or San Salvador	Guanahani	San Salvador

Index